GUARDIANS
OF THE
GALAXY
BEGINNINGS

written by *TOMAS PALACIOS*

illustrated by *RON LIM & DEAN WHITE*

MARVEL

NEW YORK / LOS ANGELES

For Sofi and Dylan.
My little Super Heroes.

Printed in the
United States of America
First Edition
1 3 5 7 9 10 8 6 4 2
G942-9090-6-14140
ISBN 978-1-4847-0054-9

Published by Marvel Press, an
imprint of Disney Book Group.
No part of this book may be
reproduced or transmitted in any
form or by any means, electronic
or mechanical, including
photocopying, recording, or
by any information storage and
retrieval system, without written
permission from the publisher.
For information address Marvel
Press, 125 West End Avenue,
New York, New York 10023.

Designed by Jennifer Redding
and John J. Hill.

marvelkids.com

SUSTAINABLE FORESTRY INITIATIVE — Certified Sourcing
www.sfiprogram.org
SFI-00993
This Label Applies to Text Stock Only

The universe is vast and beautiful. . . . And within it live both good and evil.

AND SOMETIMES... EVIL GOES LOOKING FOR A FIGHT.

That's when a group of heroes comes forth to save the day.

THESE HEROES ARE...

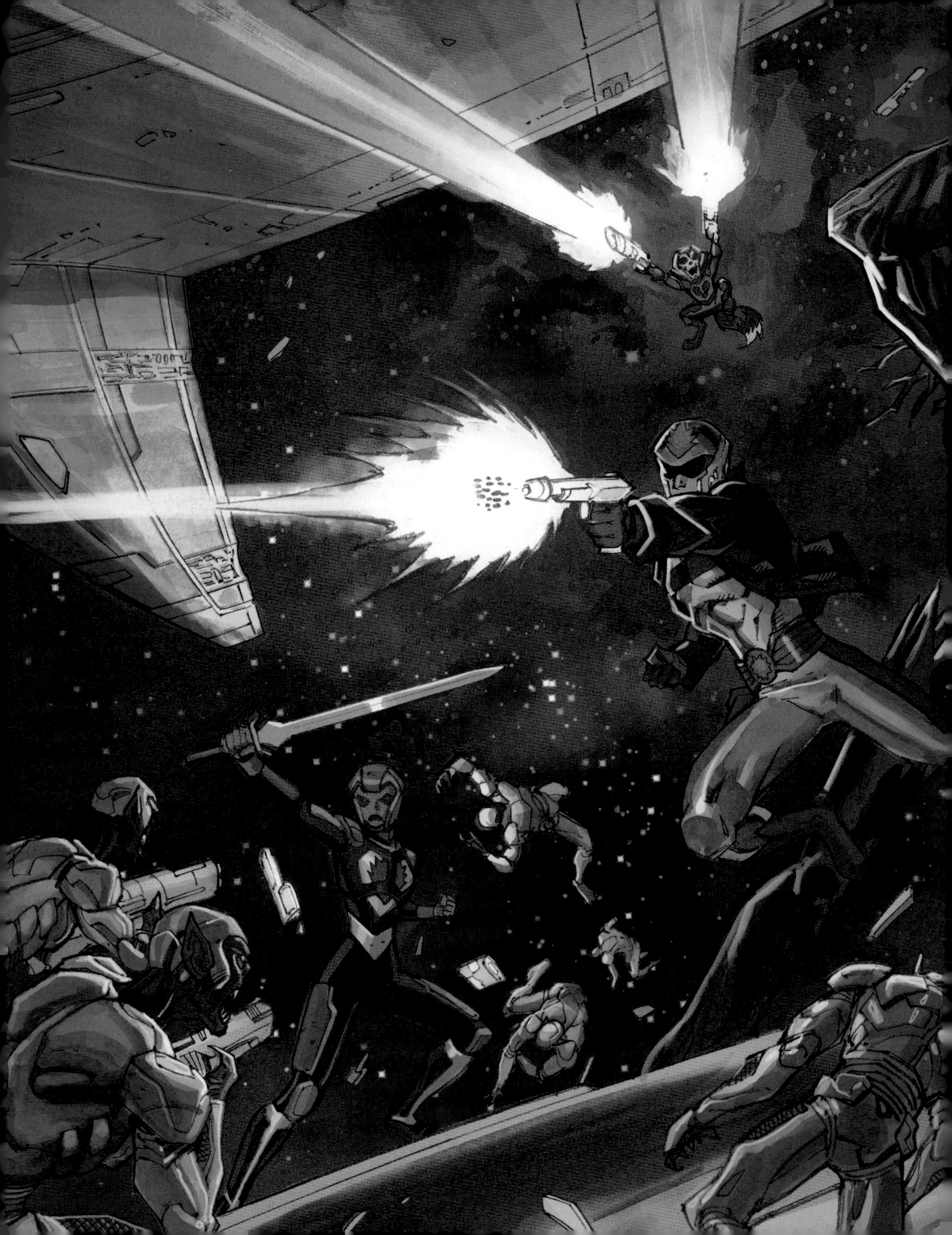

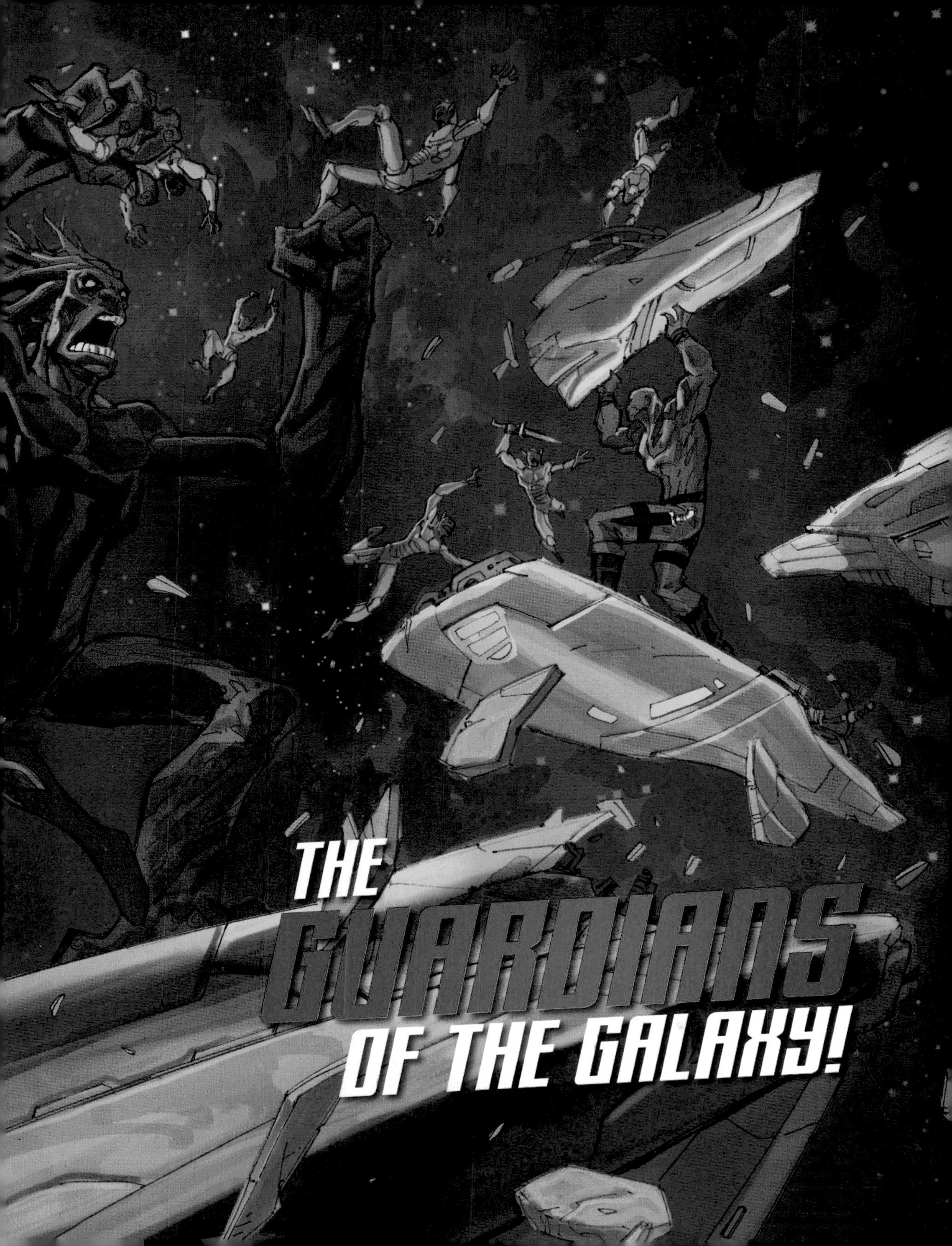
THE
GUARDIANS
OF THE GALAXY!

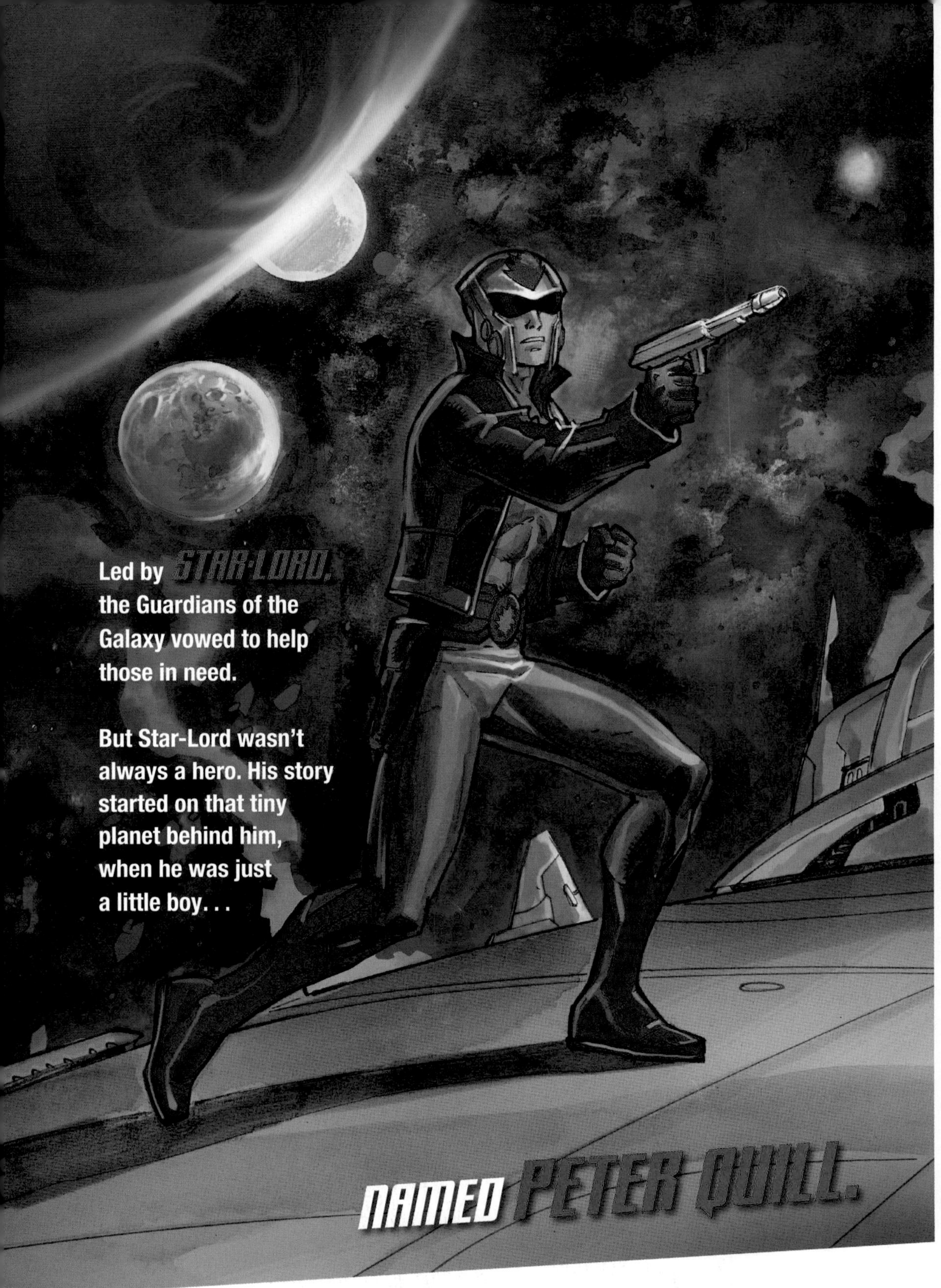

Led by **STAR-LORD,** the Guardians of the Galaxy vowed to help those in need.

But Star-Lord wasn't always a hero. His story started on that tiny planet behind him, when he was just a little boy. . .

NAMED PETER QUILL.

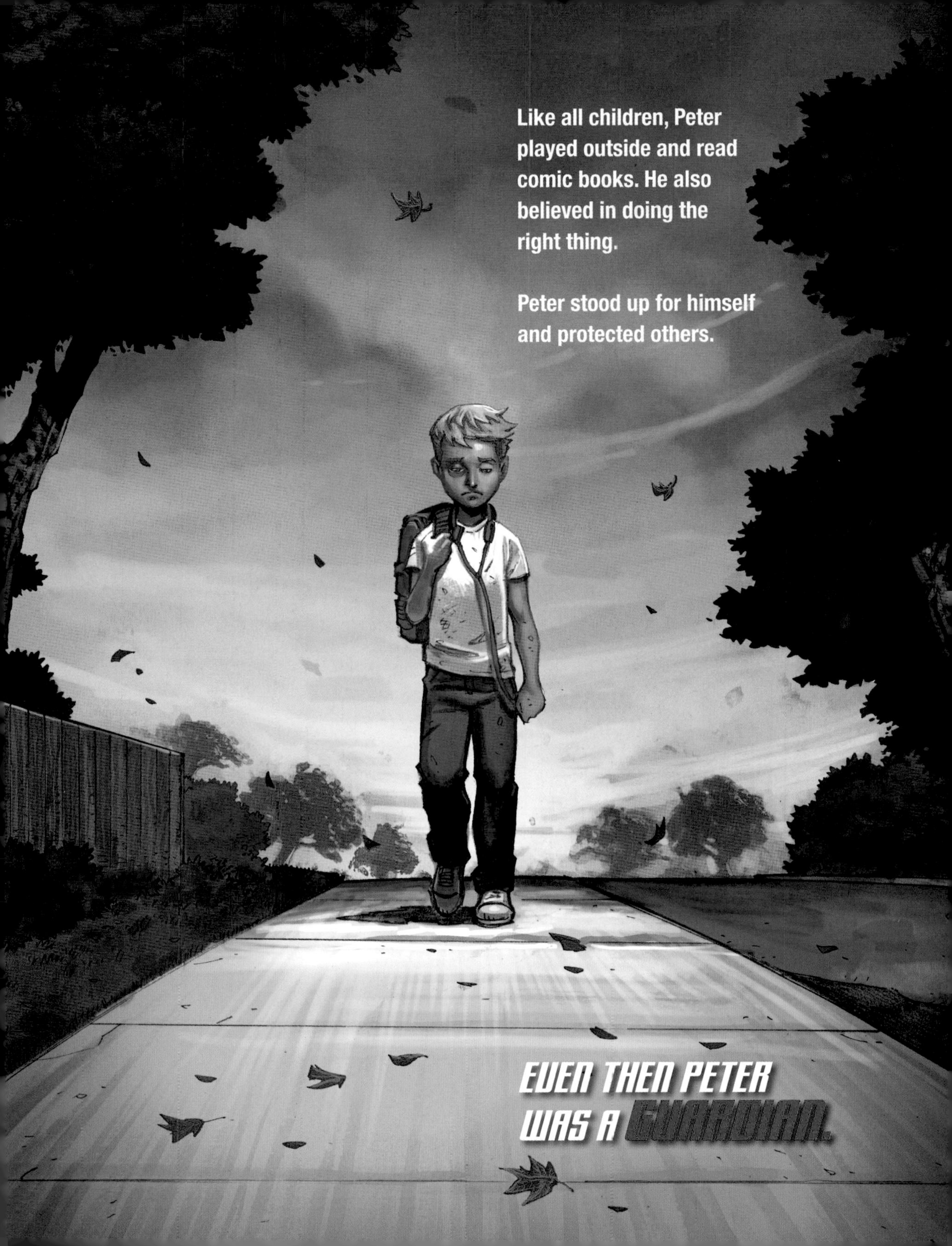
Like all children, Peter played outside and read comic books. He also believed in doing the right thing.
Peter stood up for himself and protected others.
EVEN THEN PETER WAS A GUARDIAN.

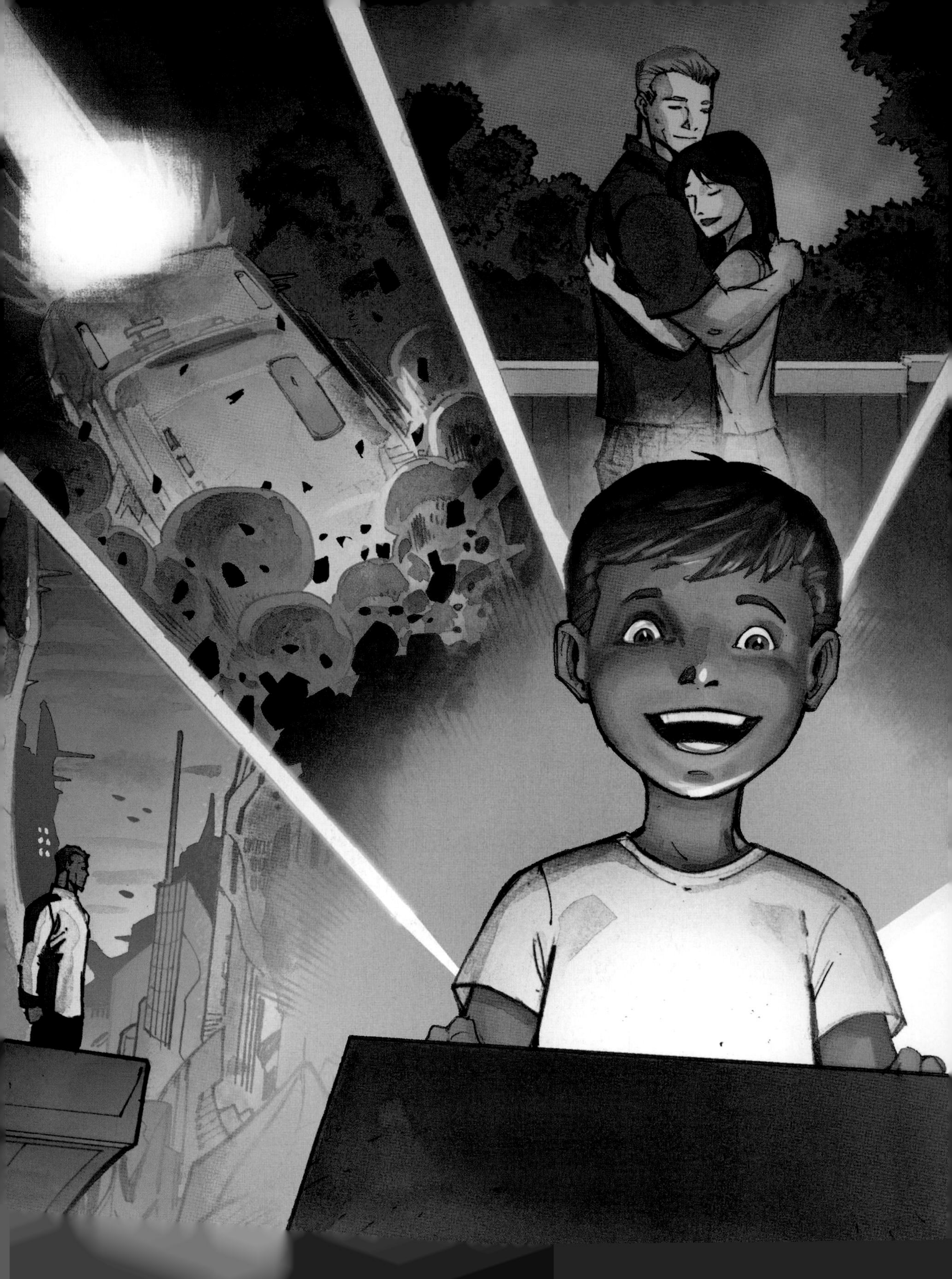

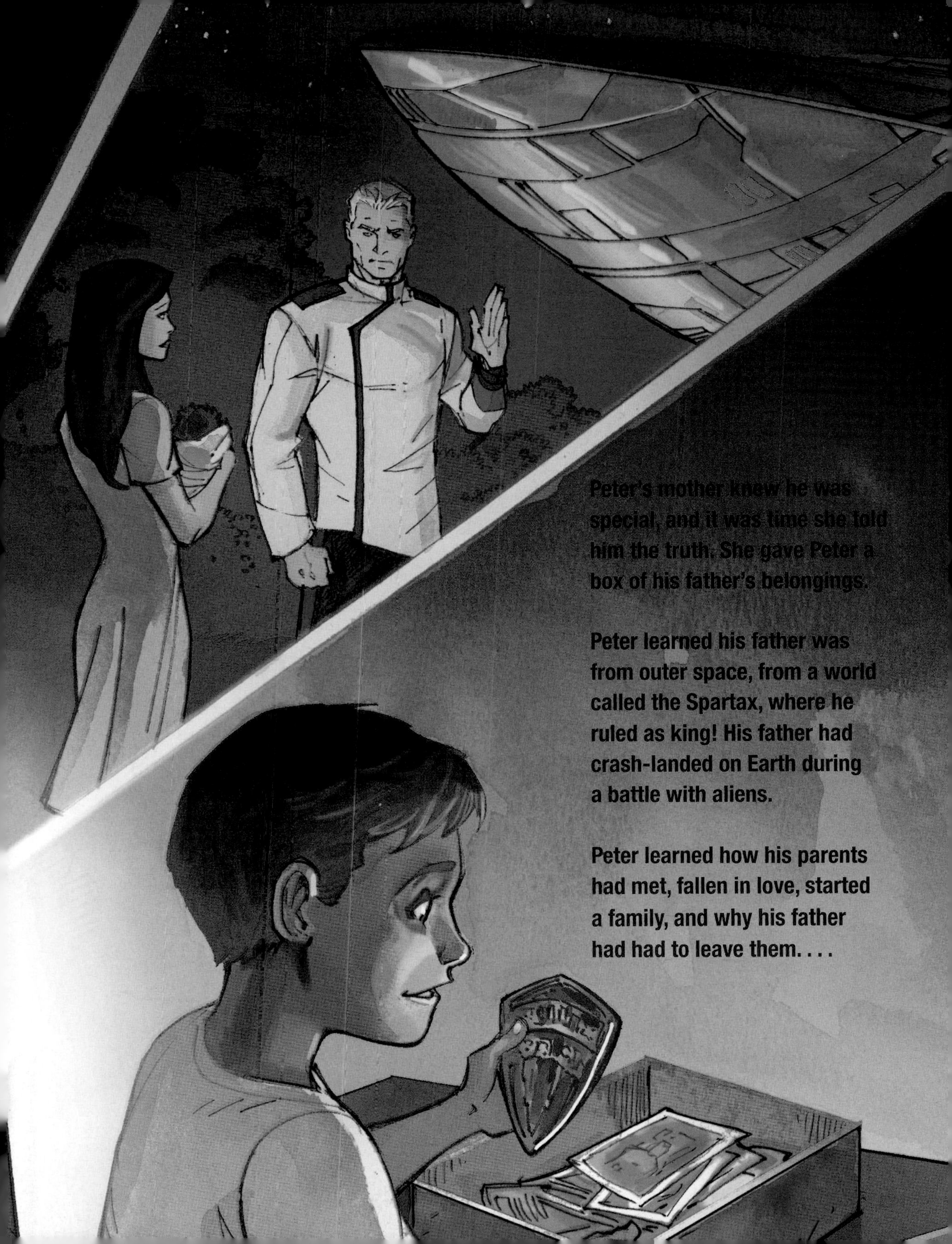

Peter's mother knew he was special, and it was time she told him the truth. She gave Peter a box of his father's belongings.

Peter learned his father was from outer space, from a world called the Spartax, where he ruled as king! His father had crash-landed on Earth during a battle with aliens.

Peter learned how his parents had met, fallen in love, started a family, and why his father had had to leave them. . . .

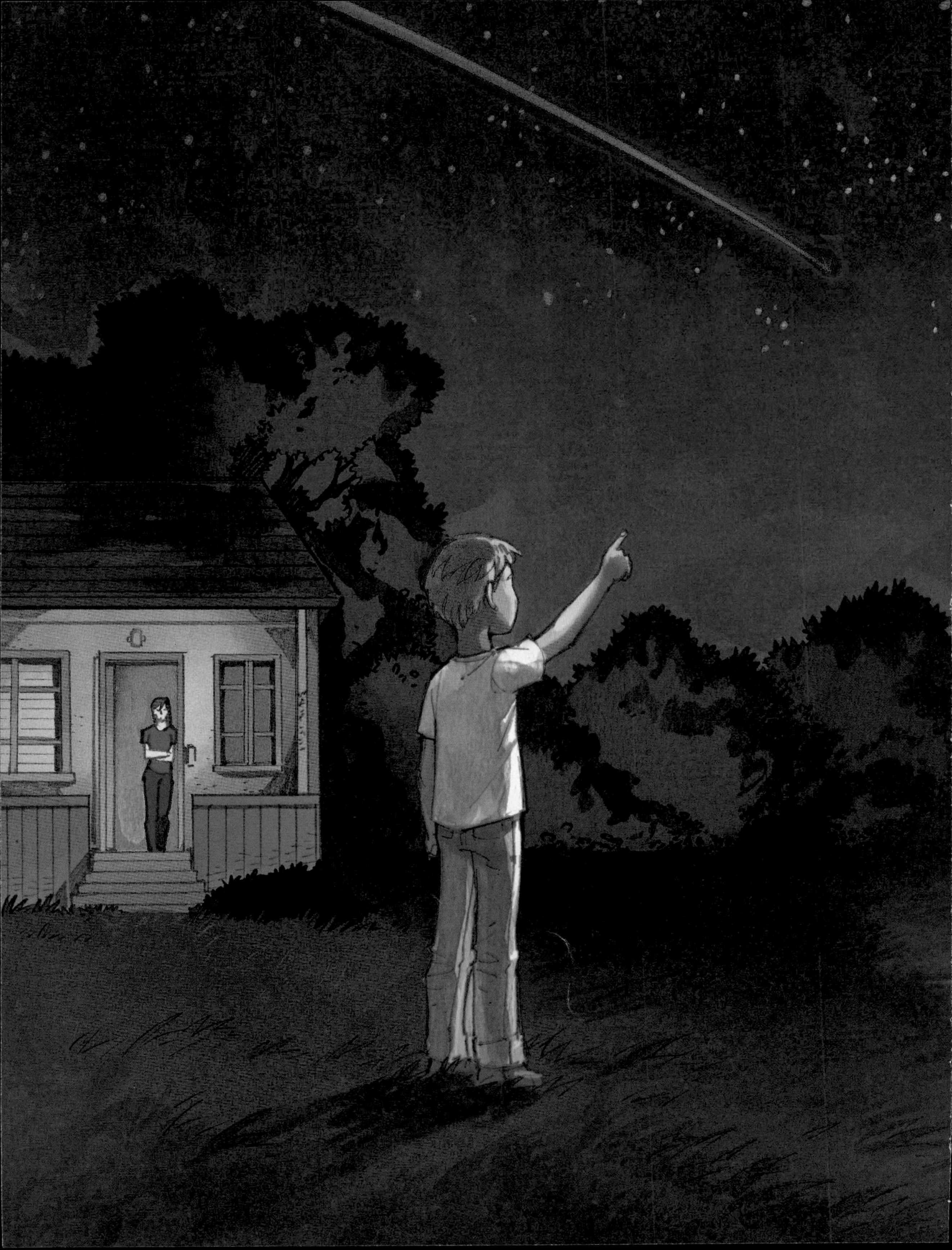

After hearing these stories, Peter decided to go find his father.

But to do so, he would have to reach for the **STARS**...

So Peter studied very hard in school, learning as much as he could about planets, moons, and galaxies!

Eventually, Peter earned a scholarship and went to college!

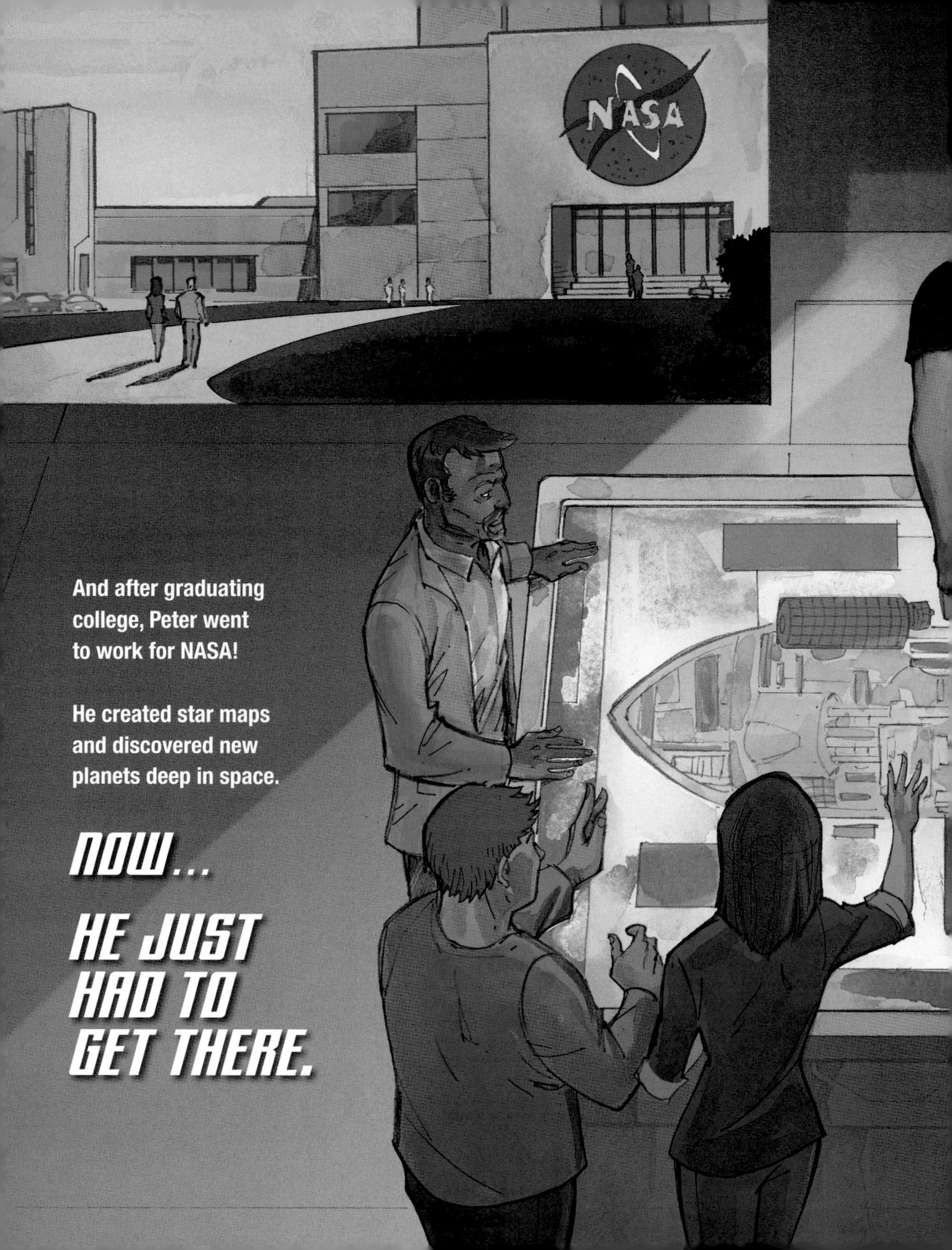
NASA
And after graduating college, Peter went to work for NASA!
He created star maps and discovered new planets deep in space.
NOW...
HE JUST HAD TO GET THERE.

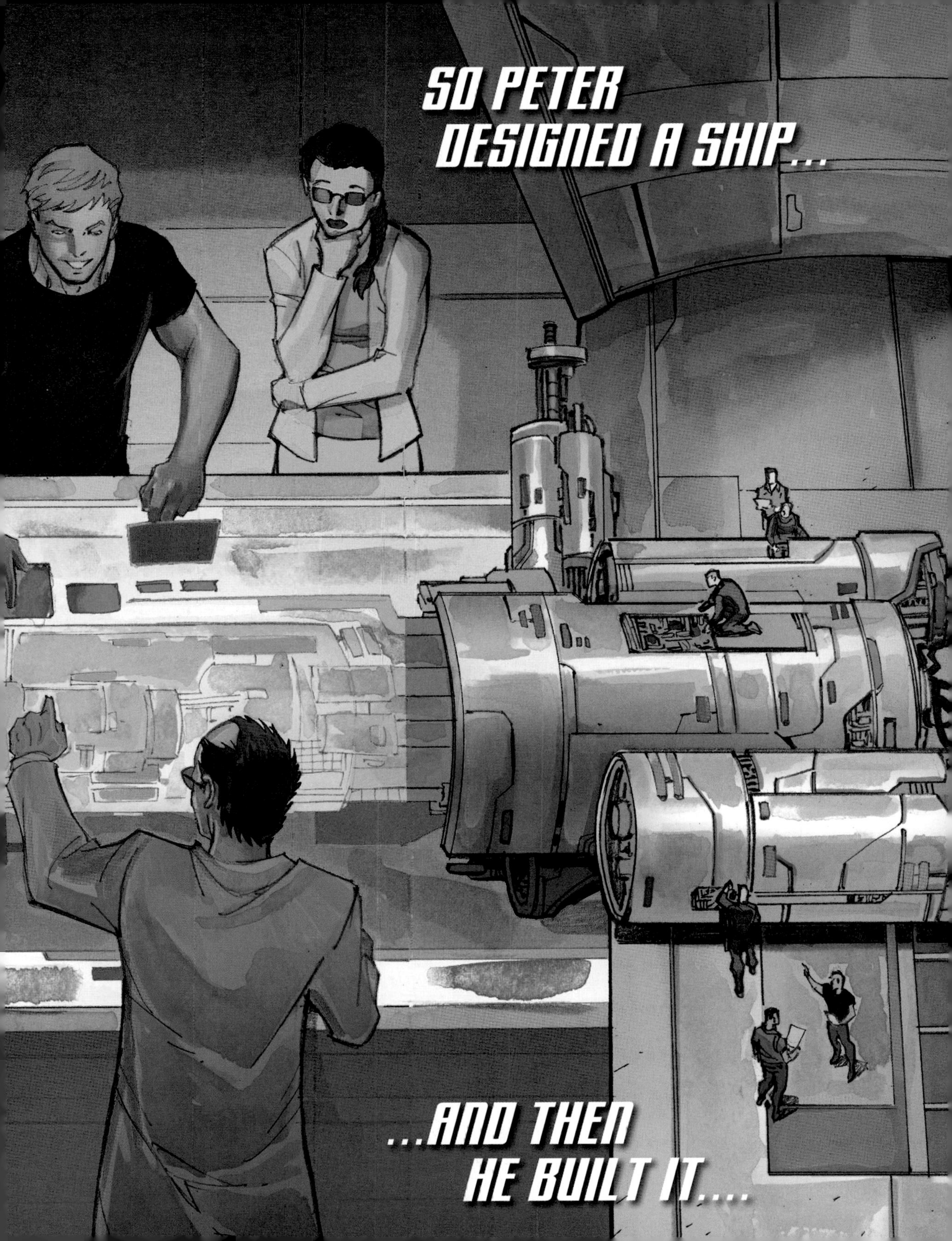
SO PETER
DESIGNED A SHIP...
...AND THEN
HE BUILT IT....

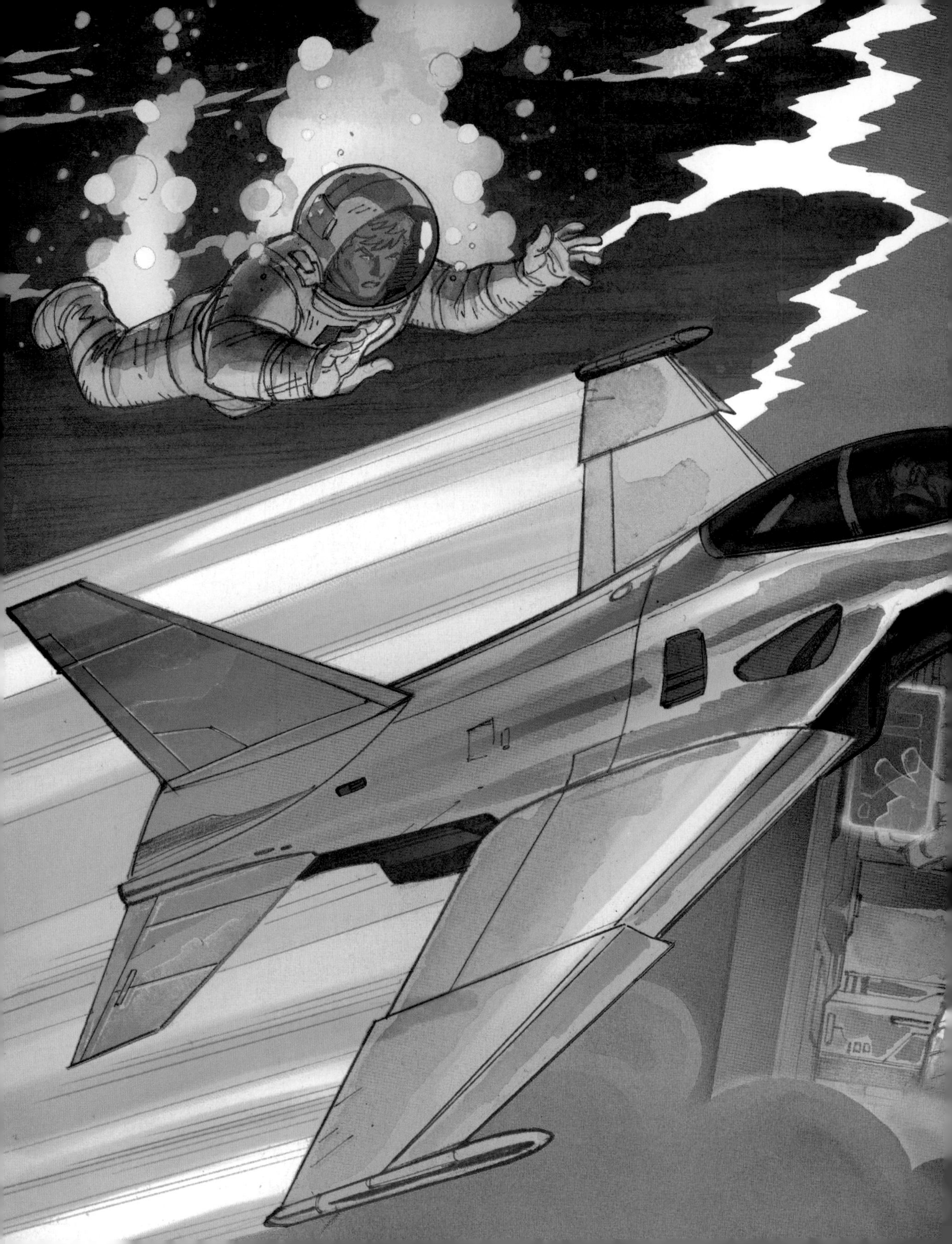
100

Peter began to prepare for space. He learned about gravity and how to fly, and after much practice and many, many years of hard work, Peter became an astronaut!

HE WAS FINALLY READY TO FIND HIS DAD!

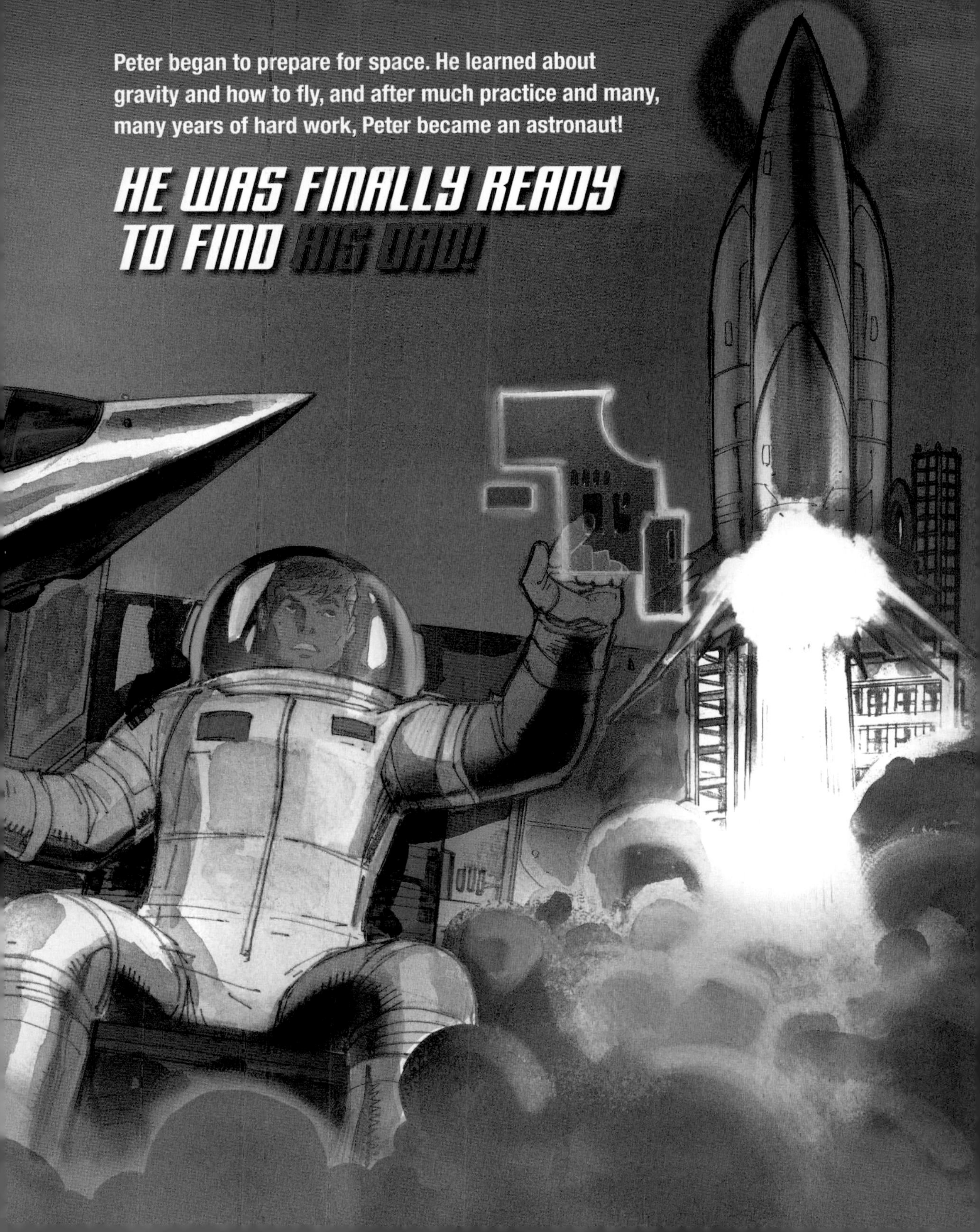

Peter's mother did not know her son's future, but she knew that he would be safe. After all, he was the son of an intergalactic fighter!

PETER BLASTED OFF INTO THE SKY!

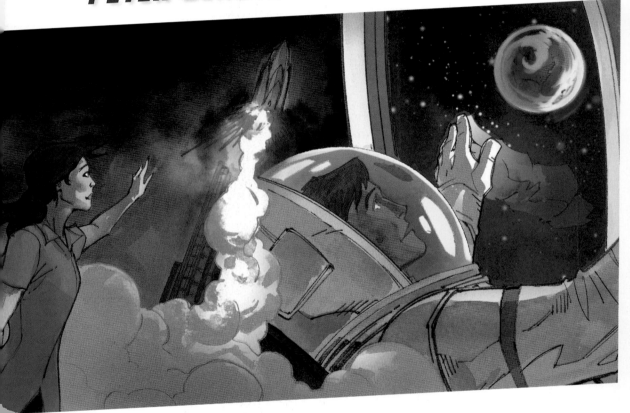

He broke through Earth's atmosphere, rocketing into space, past the stars and past the moon!

Peter looked back at Earth as it became smaller and smaller. Now it was just him, his ship, and the galaxy.

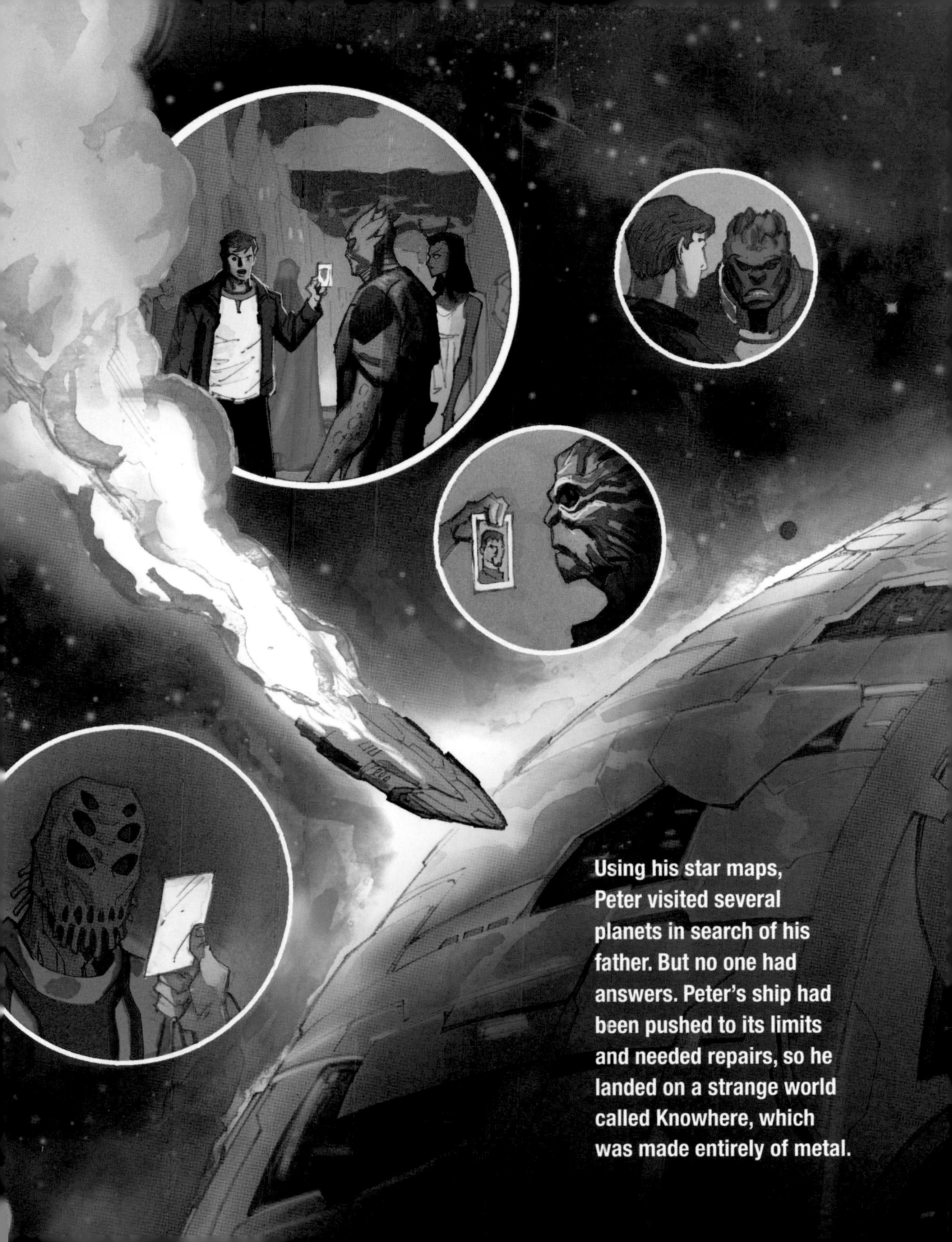

Using his star maps, Peter visited several planets in search of his father. But no one had answers. Peter's ship had been pushed to its limits and needed repairs, so he landed on a strange world called Knowhere, which was made entirely of metal.

As he roamed the planet, Peter learned that a great intergalactic king had arrived. The king and his fleet of soldiers approached Peter.

INSTEAD OF PETER FINDING HIS DAD...

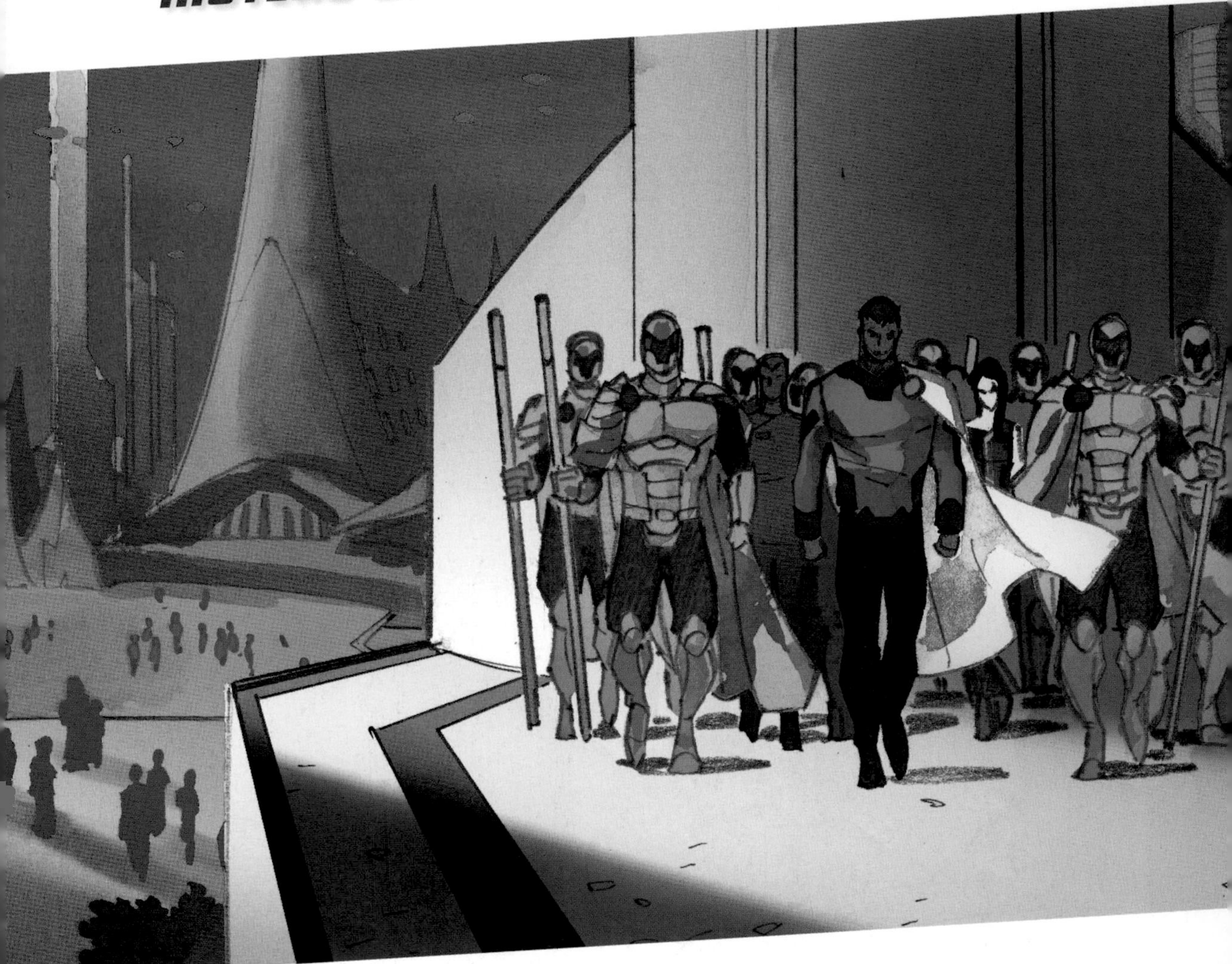

PETER'S DAD HAD FOUND HIM.

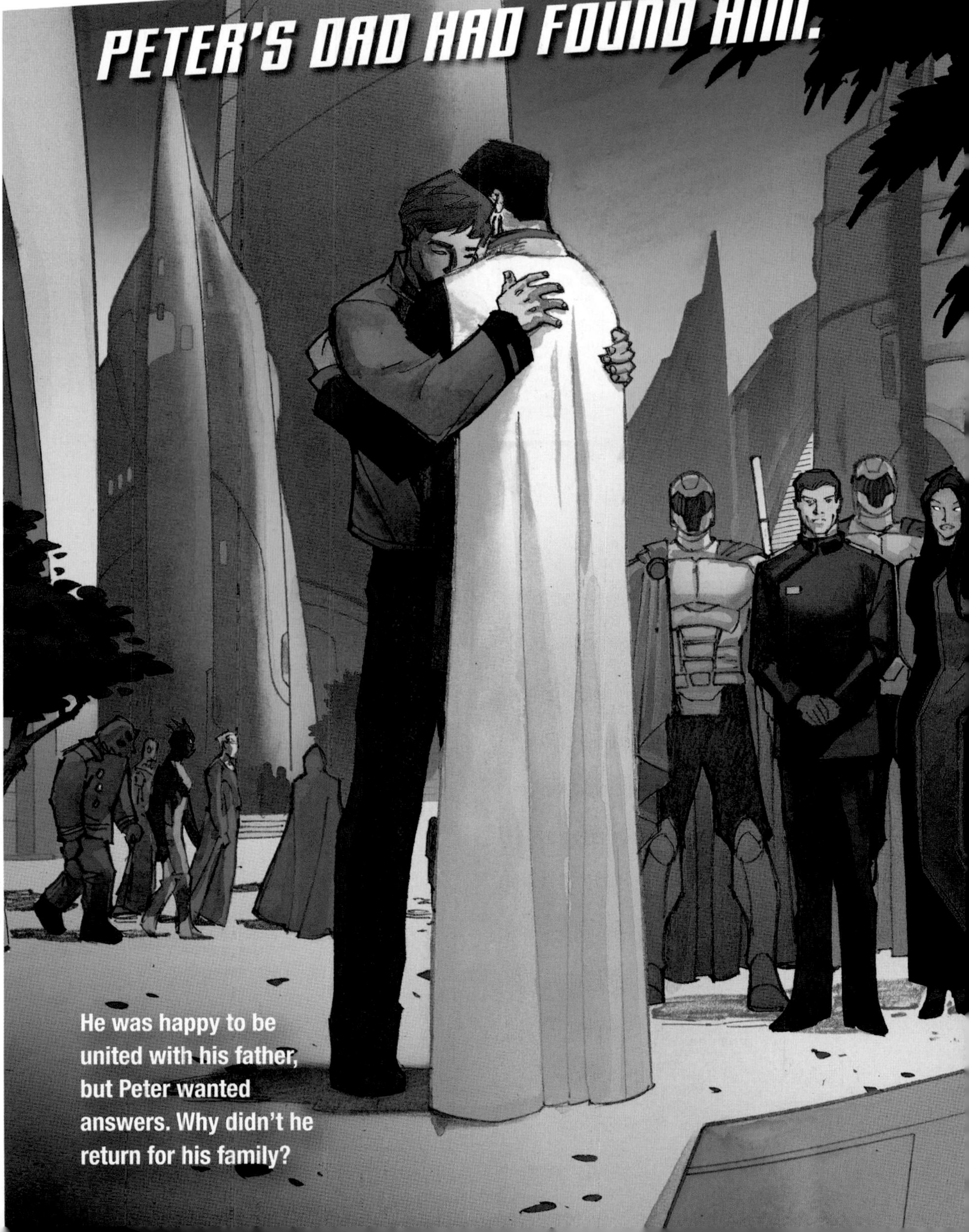

He was happy to be united with his father, but Peter wanted answers. Why didn't he return for his family?

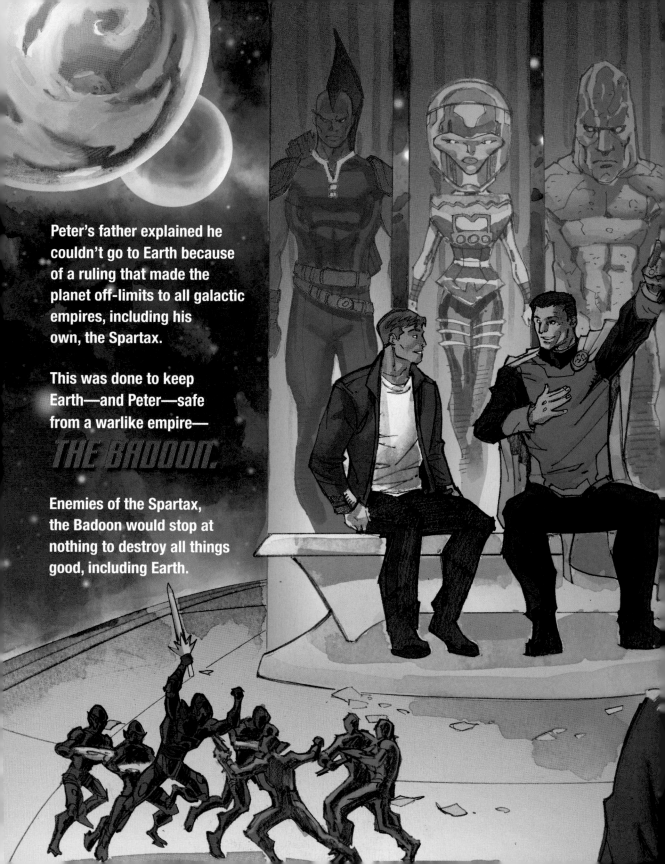

Peter's father explained he couldn't go to Earth because of a ruling that made the planet off-limits to all galactic empires, including his own, the Spartax.

This was done to keep Earth—and Peter—safe from a warlike empire—

THE BADOON.

Enemies of the Spartax, the Badoon would stop at nothing to destroy all things good, including Earth.

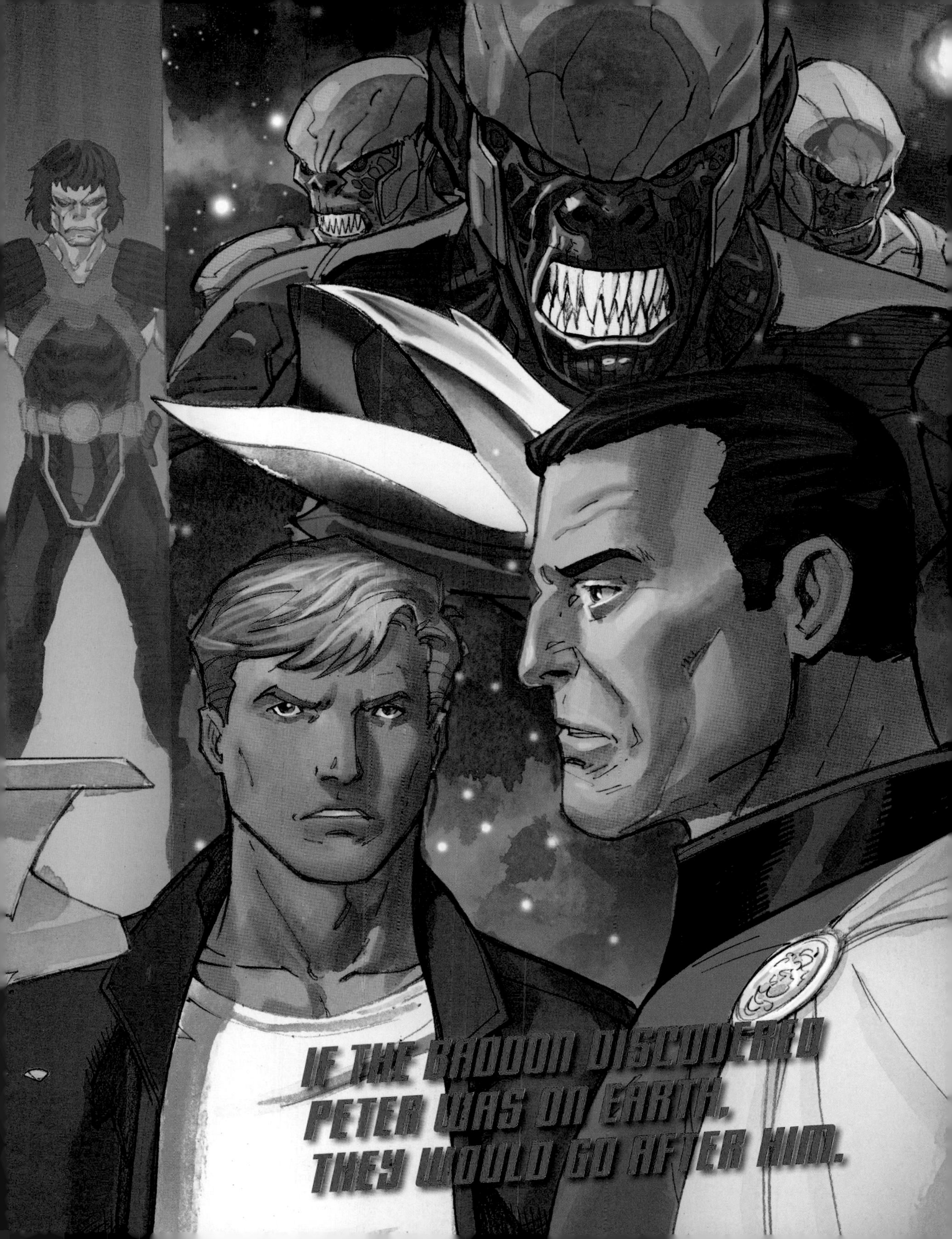
IF THE BADOON DISCOVERED
PETER WAS ON EARTH,
THEY WOULD GO AFTER HIM.

He gave Peter a ship, called the *Milano*, and special armor, that empowered him.

PETER COULD RUN FASTER, BECOME STRONGER, AND EVEN FLY!

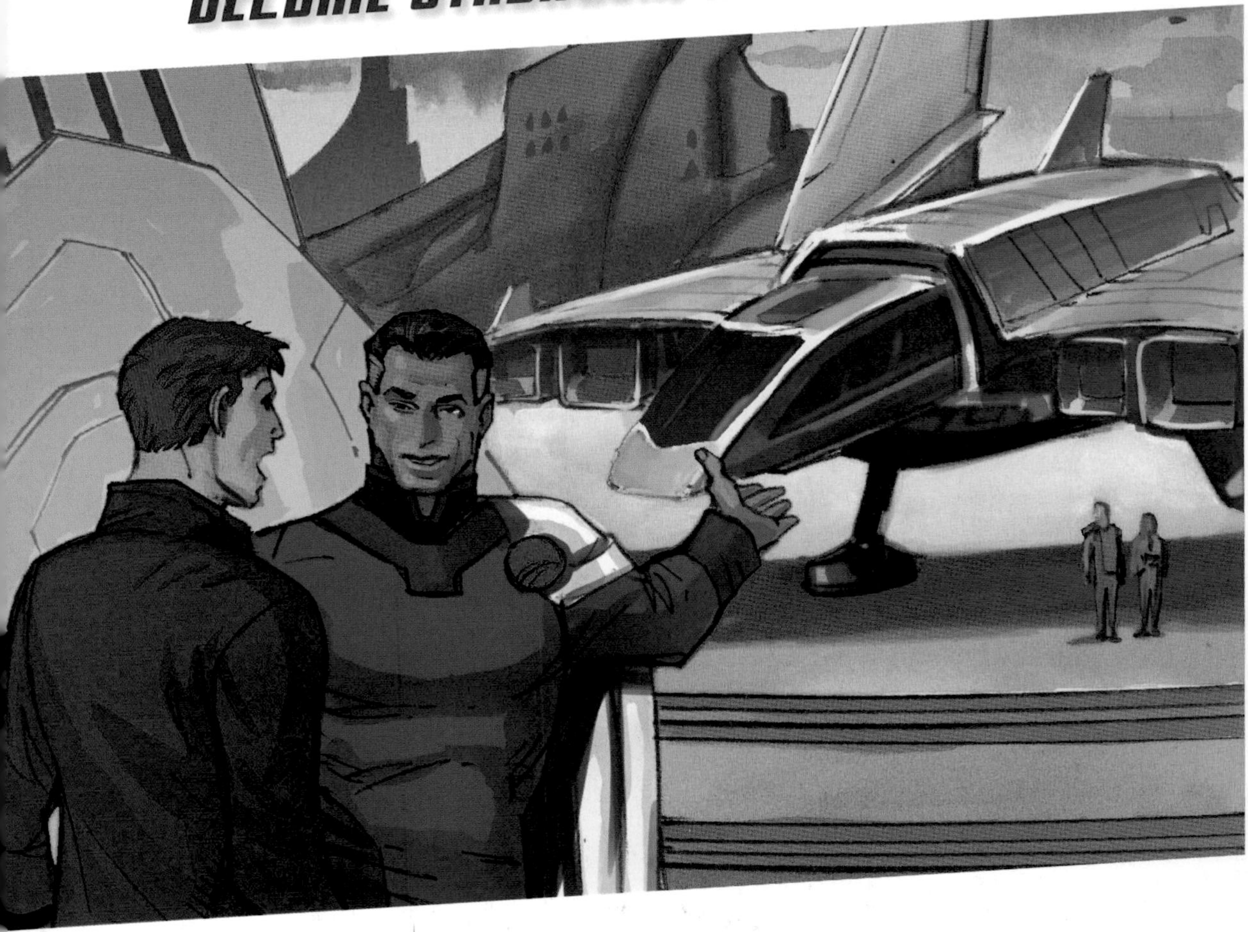

Peter thought about how far he had come to find his father. He knew if he ever wanted to see his family united, he would have to stay and fight the Badoon. From that day forth Peter Quill would be known throughout the Galaxy as. . .

STAR-LORD!

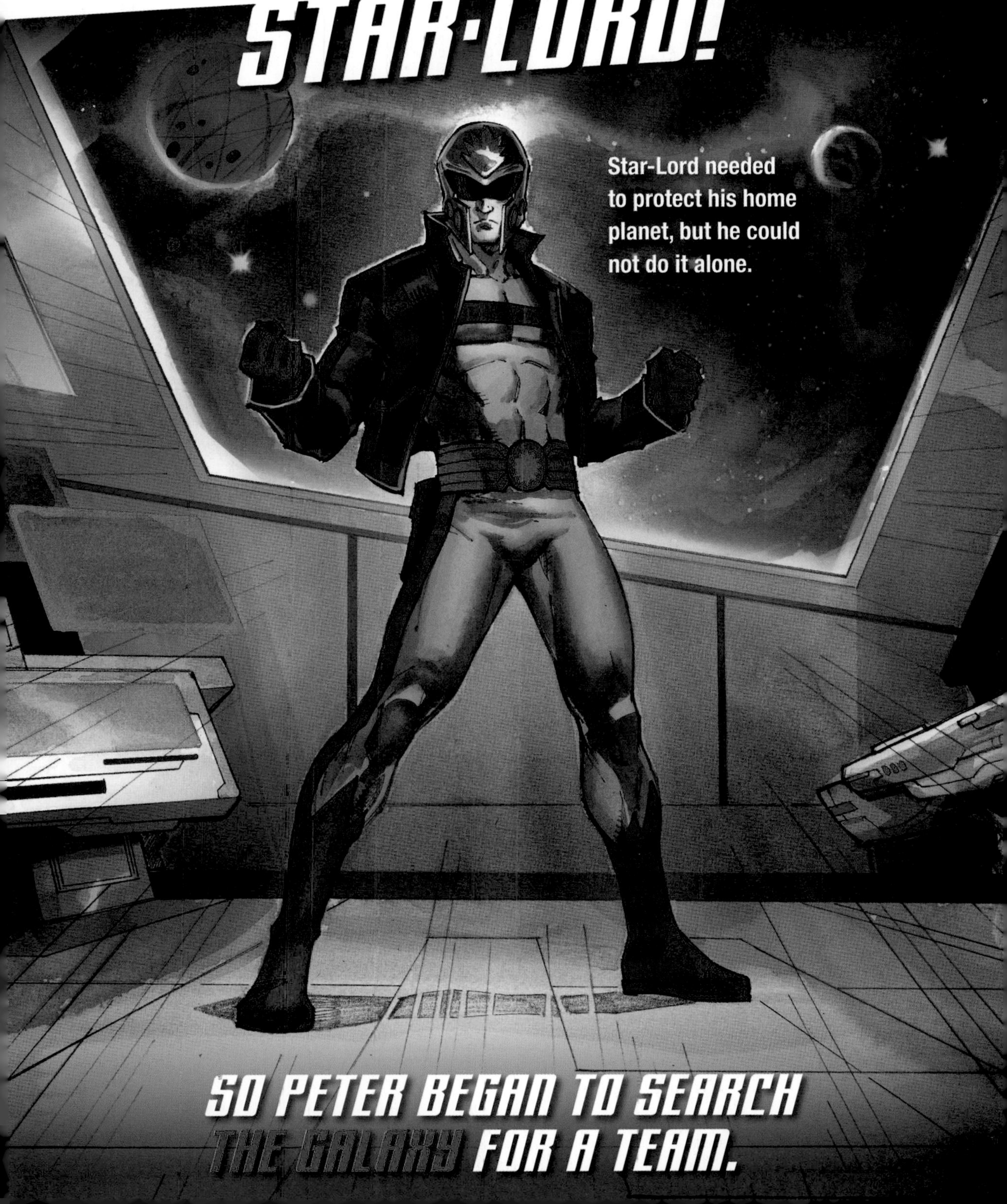

Star-Lord needed to protect his home planet, but he could not do it alone.

SO PETER BEGAN TO SEARCH THE GALAXY FOR A TEAM.

First he met

GAMORA!

With her people enslaved and her village destroyed by the Badoon, young Gamora fled her planet. She was very young—and very scared.

Taken in by Thanos, the most feared villain in the universe, Gamora was raised to be a dangerous warrior.

But after many years, Gamora realized Thanos was just like the Badoon, so she fled once again, vowing always to fight evil.

GAMORA AGREED TO JOIN STAR-LORD.

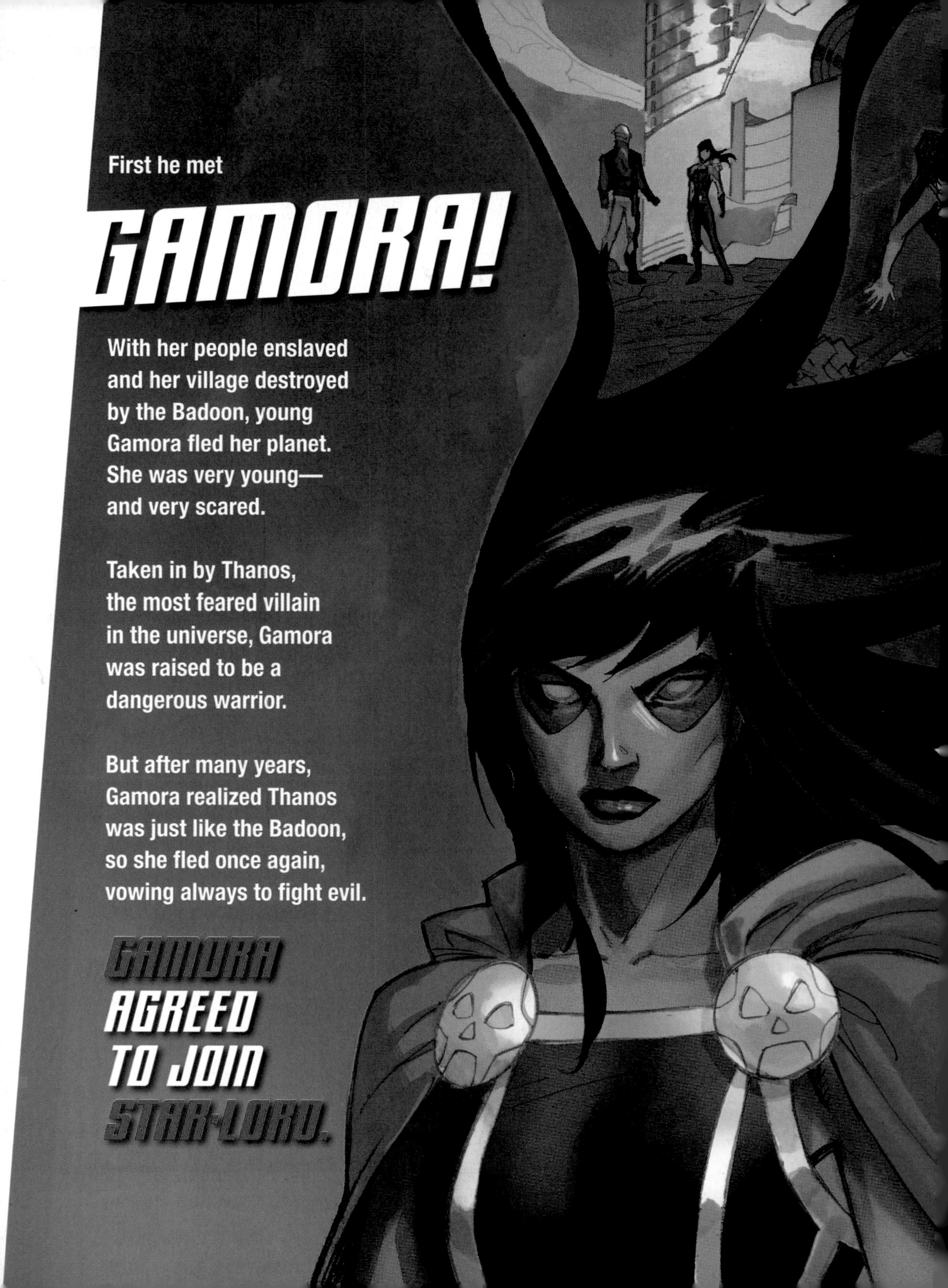

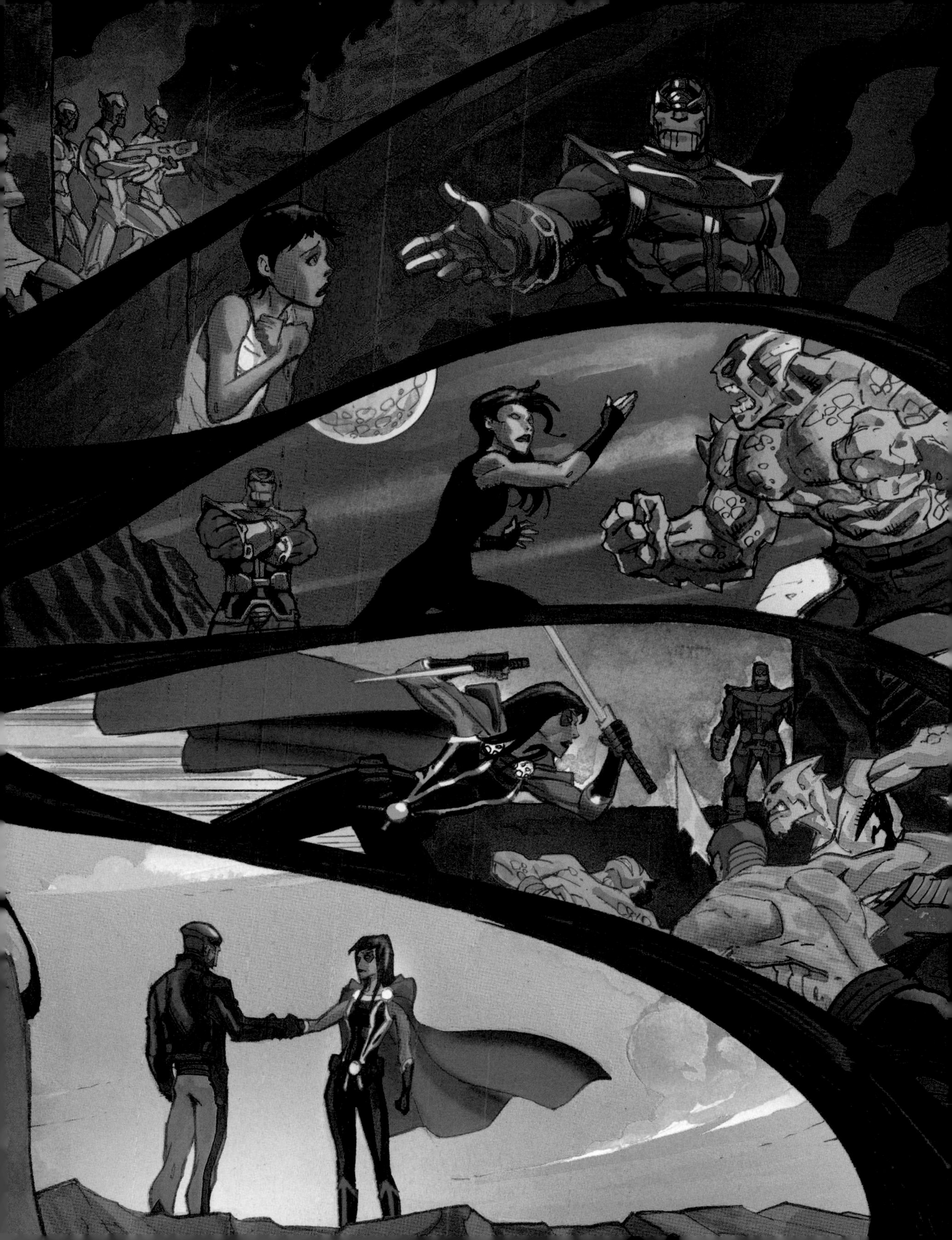

Gamora told Star-Lord of a great warrior named. . .

DRAX THE DESTROYER!

Legend had it that Drax became so enraged when he lost his family to the Badoon that he defeated one of their fighter ships all by himself!

Since then, Drax has traveled the galaxy, fighting for good, living by his own moral code, and desiring peace for everyone. Knowing what it was like to lose a family,

DRAX AGREED TO JOIN STAR-LORD AND GAMORA.

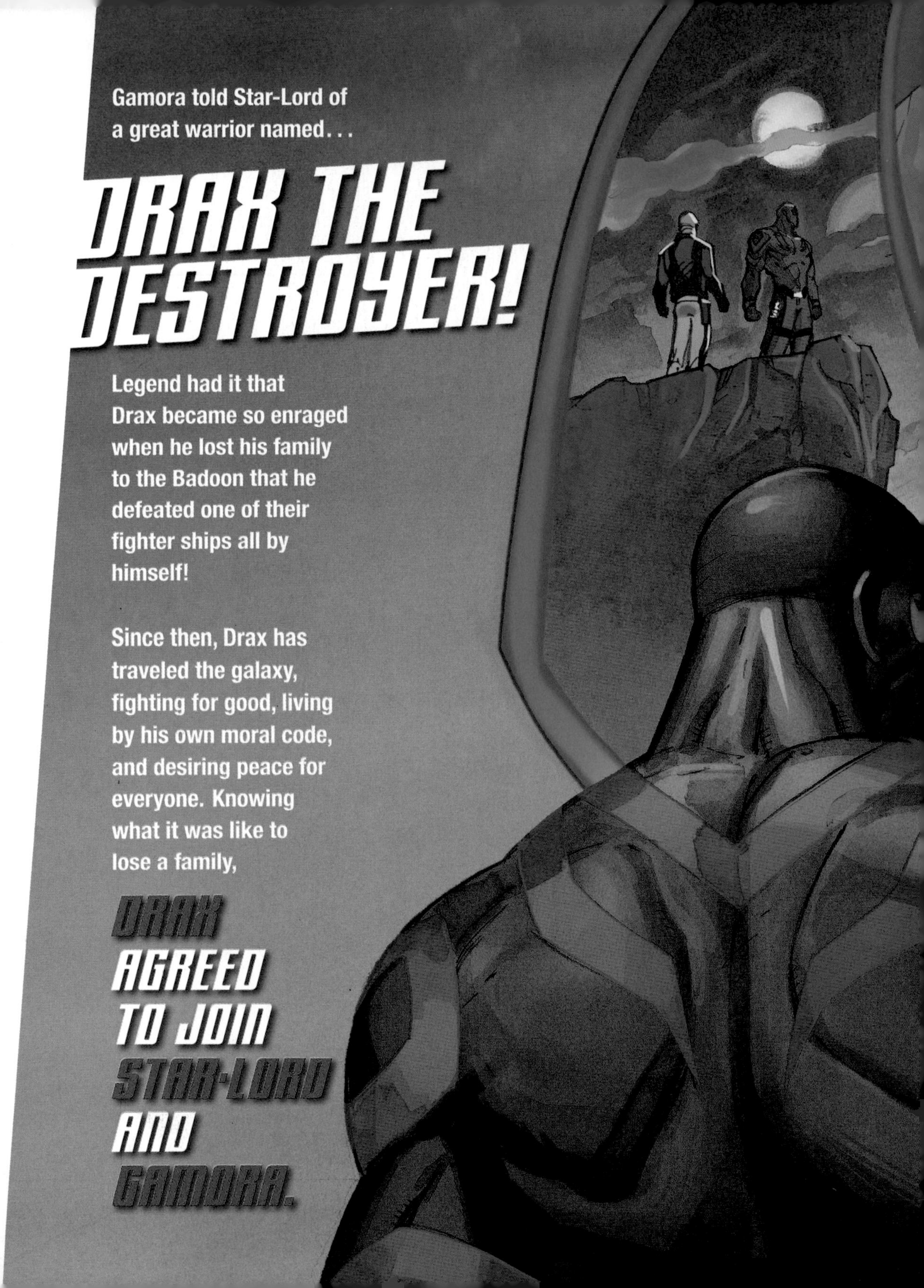

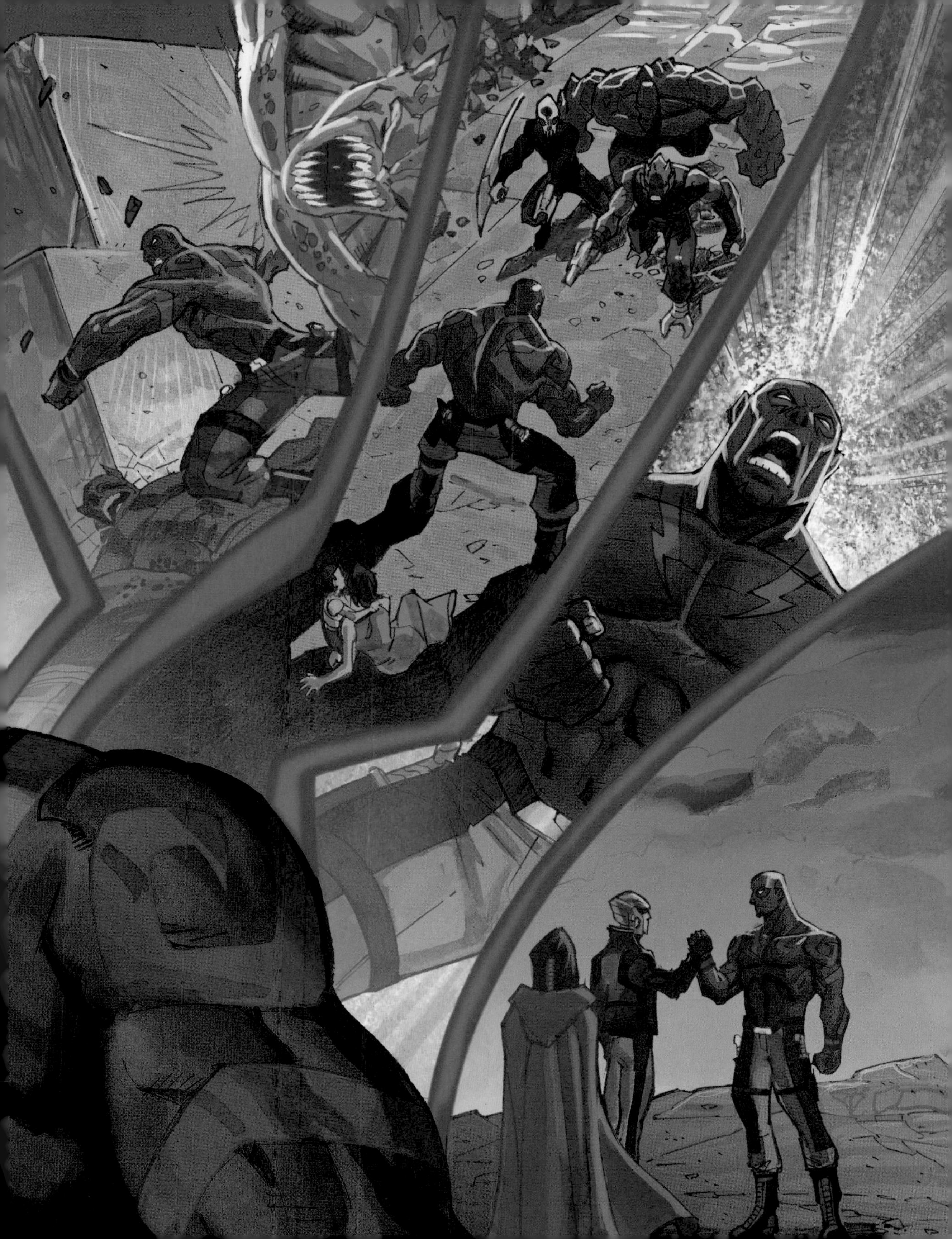

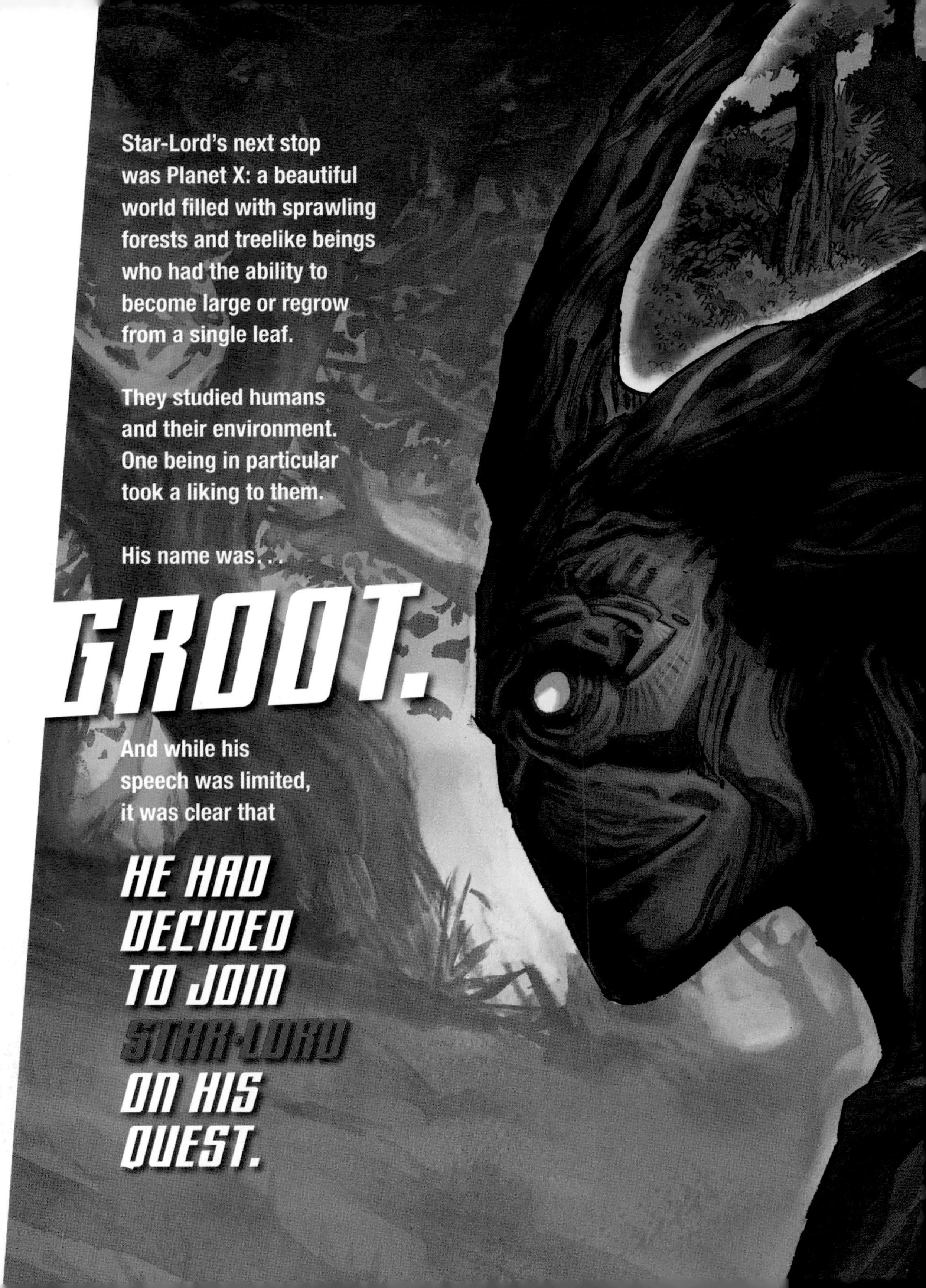

Star-Lord's next stop was Planet X: a beautiful world filled with sprawling forests and treelike beings who had the ability to become large or regrow from a single leaf.

They studied humans and their environment. One being in particular took a liking to them.

His name was. . .

GROOT.

And while his speech was limited, it was clear that

HE HAD DECIDED TO JOIN STAR-LORD ON HIS QUEST.

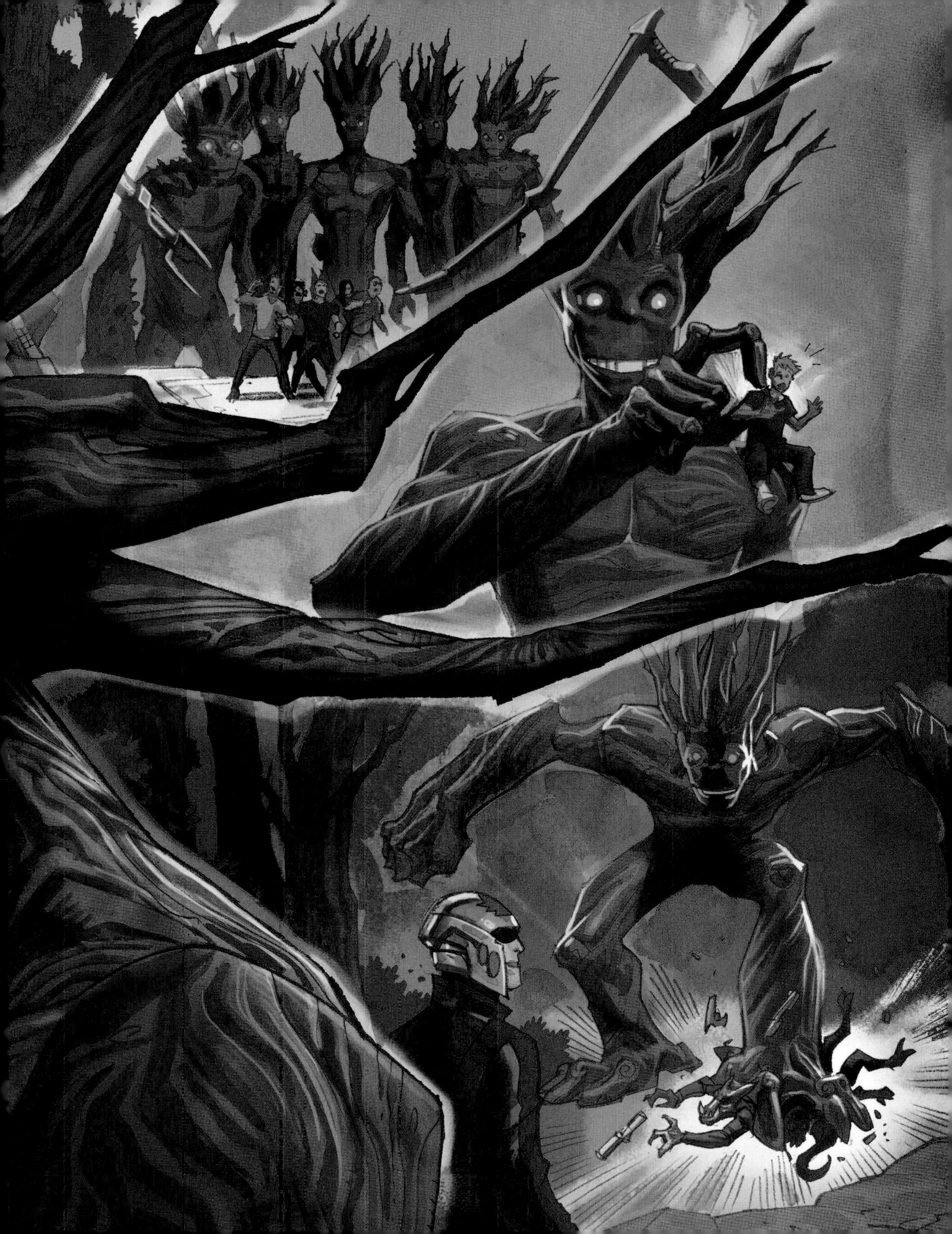

Star-Lord's last stop was the planet Halfworld to find the one named

ROCKET RACCOON!

He was no ordinary raccoon. They found him atop a pile of defeated aliens, ready for his next battle.

He was born a fierce fighter. Scientists noticed this and gave him advanced skills. "Rocket" learned to use his new talents on what he loved to do best: make new weapons! And firing them at the bad guys was his specialty!

SO, ROCKET JOINED STAR-LORD AND HIS TEAM.

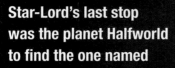

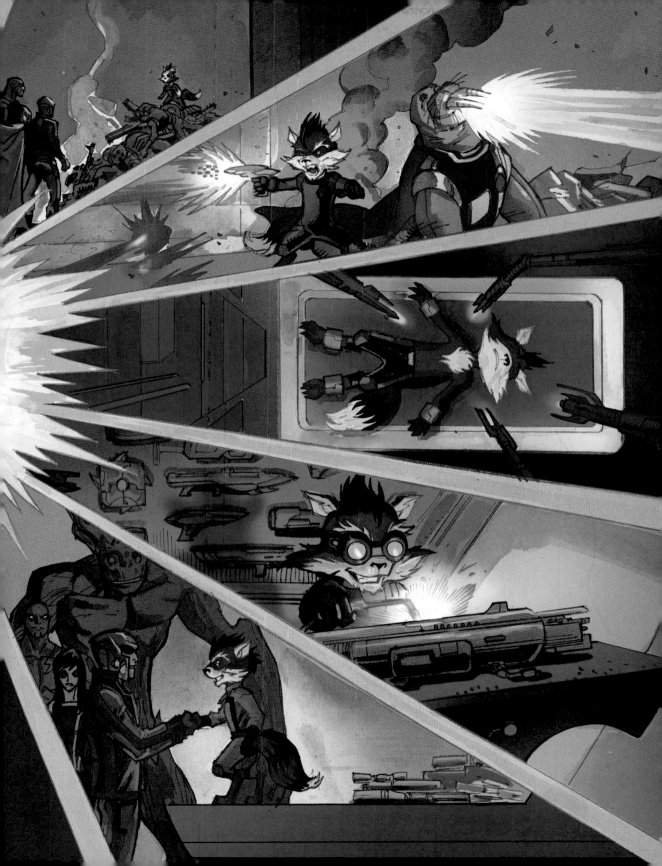

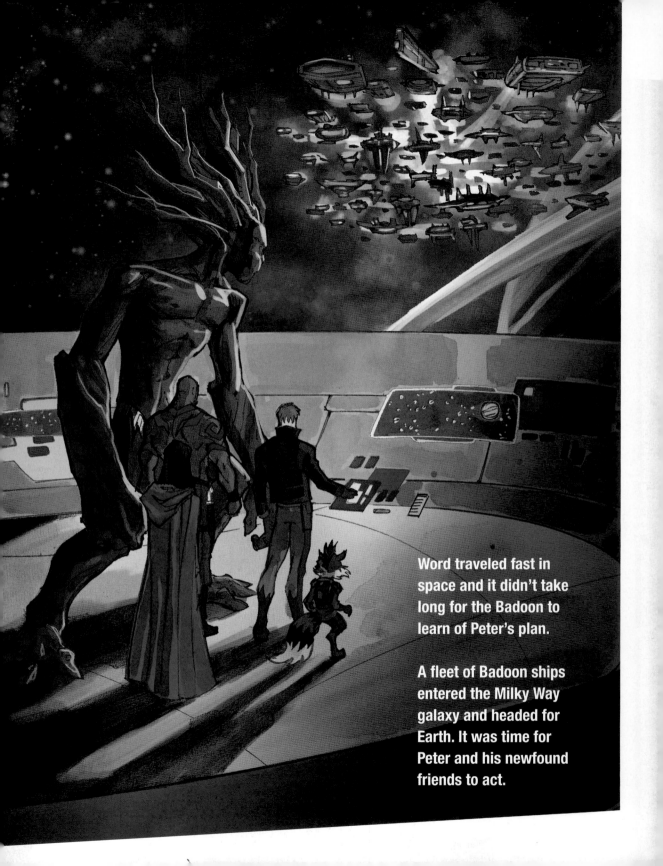

Word traveled fast in space and it didn't take long for the Badoon to learn of Peter's plan.

A fleet of Badoon ships entered the Milky Way galaxy and headed for Earth. It was time for Peter and his newfound friends to act.

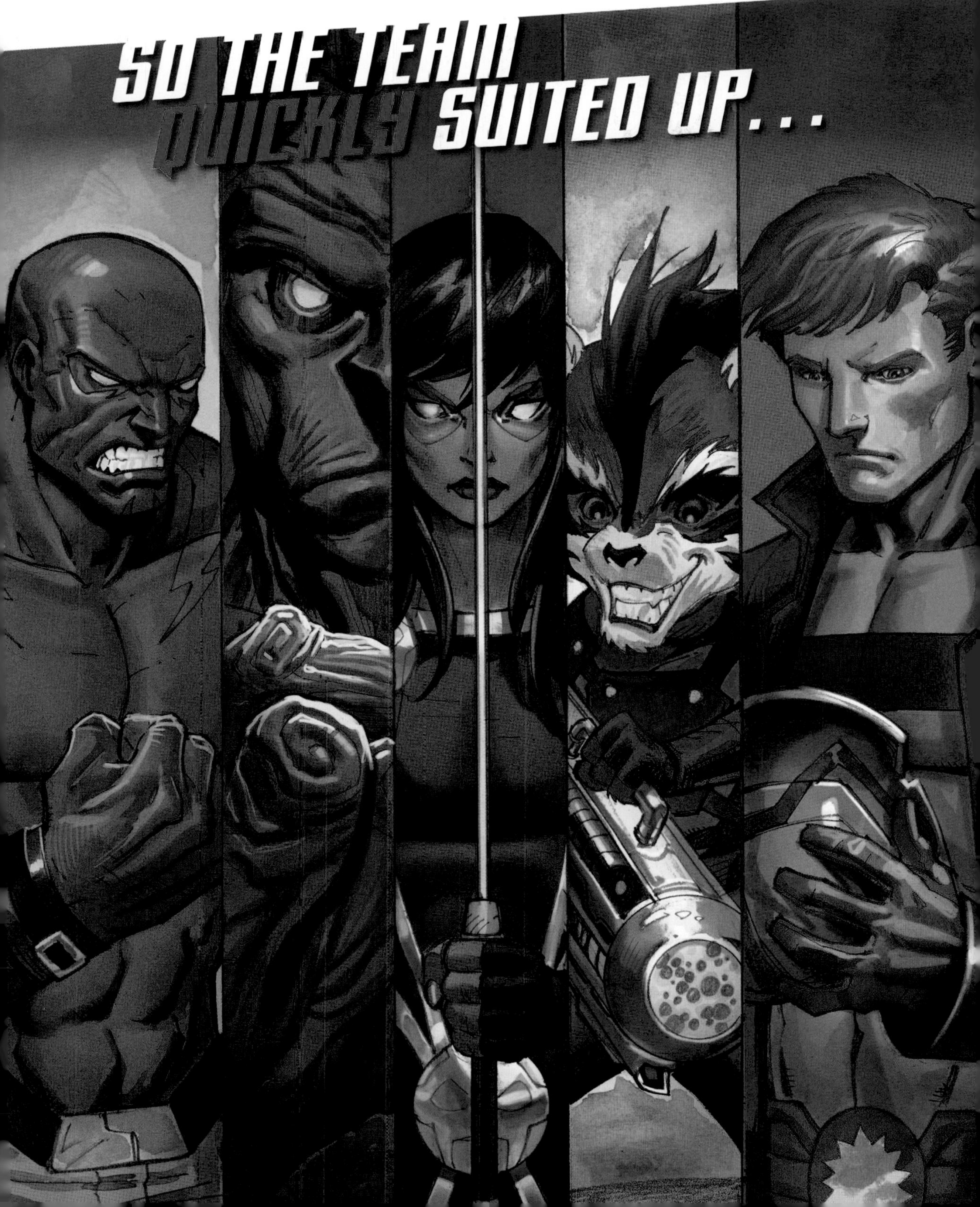
SO THE TEAM QUICKLY SUITED UP...

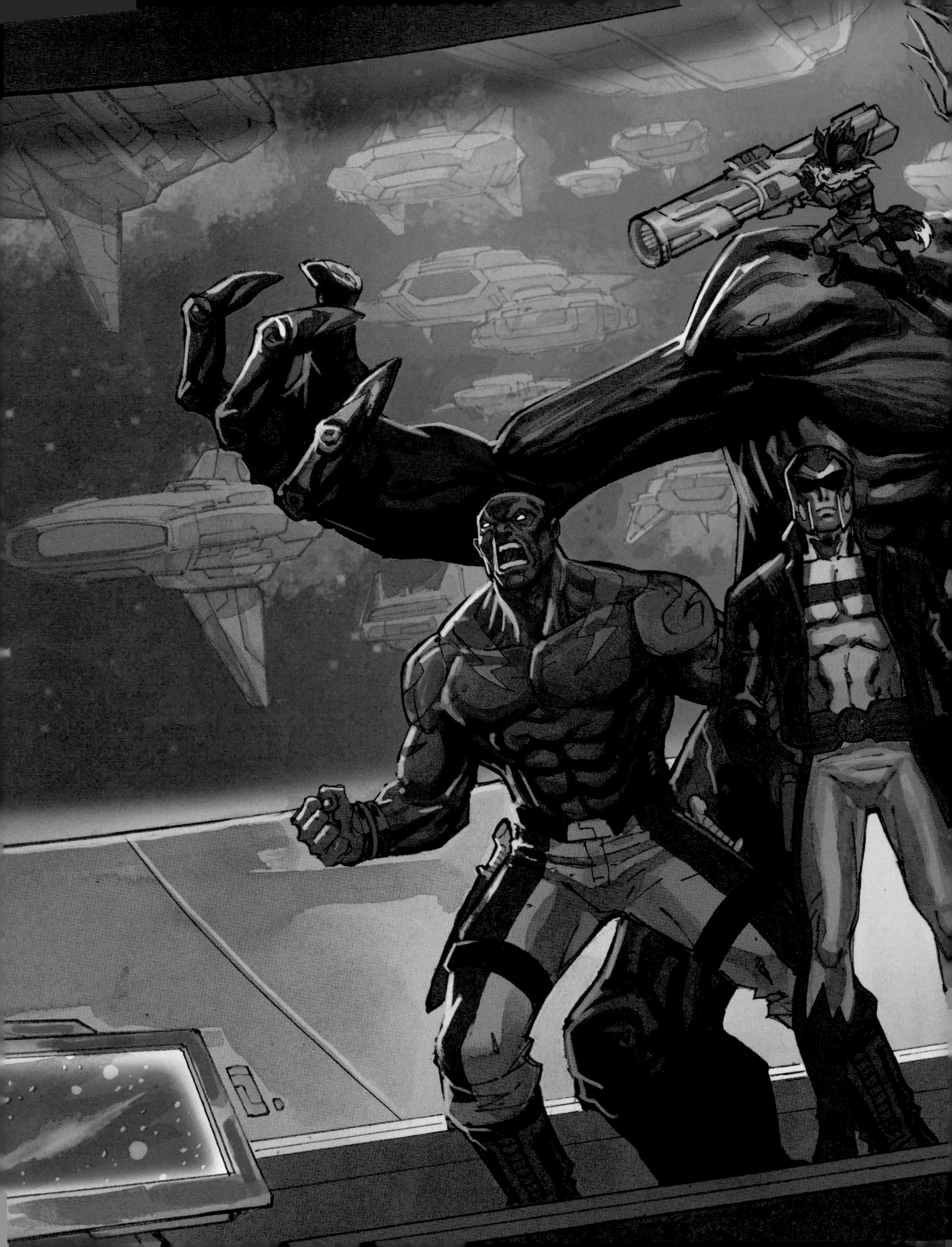

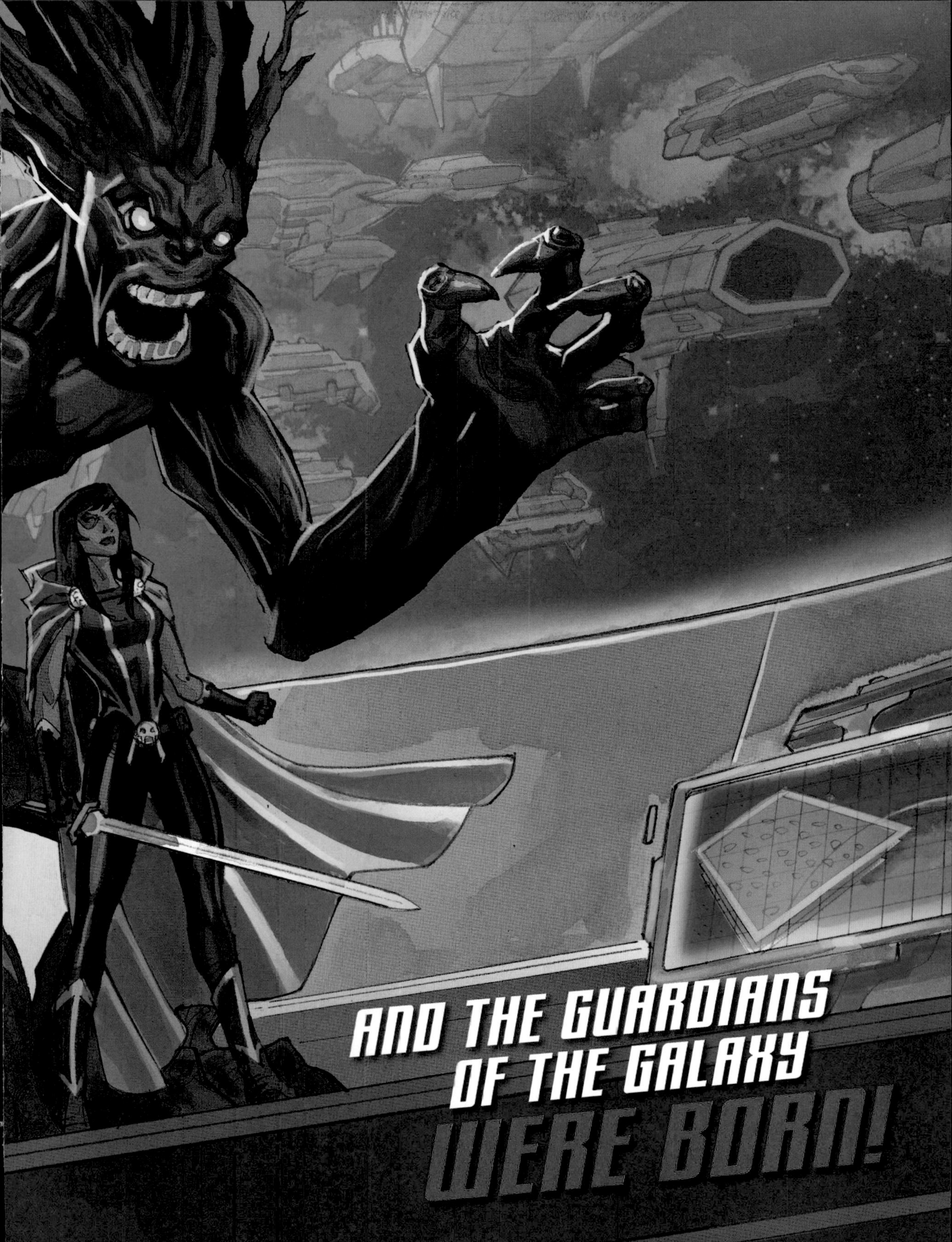
AND THE GUARDIANS
OF THE GALAXY
WERE BORN!

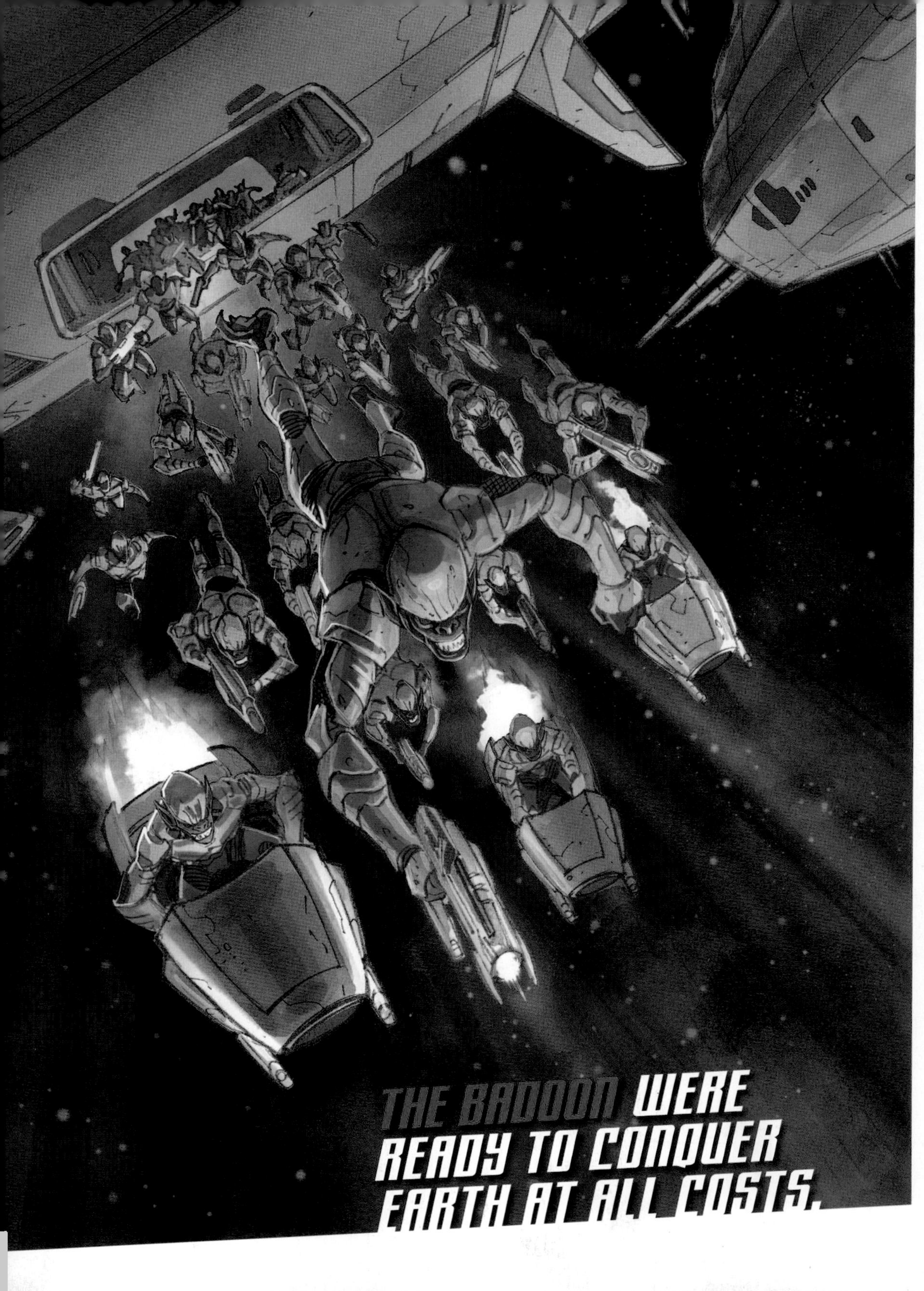
THE BADOON WERE READY TO CONQUER EARTH AT ALL COSTS.

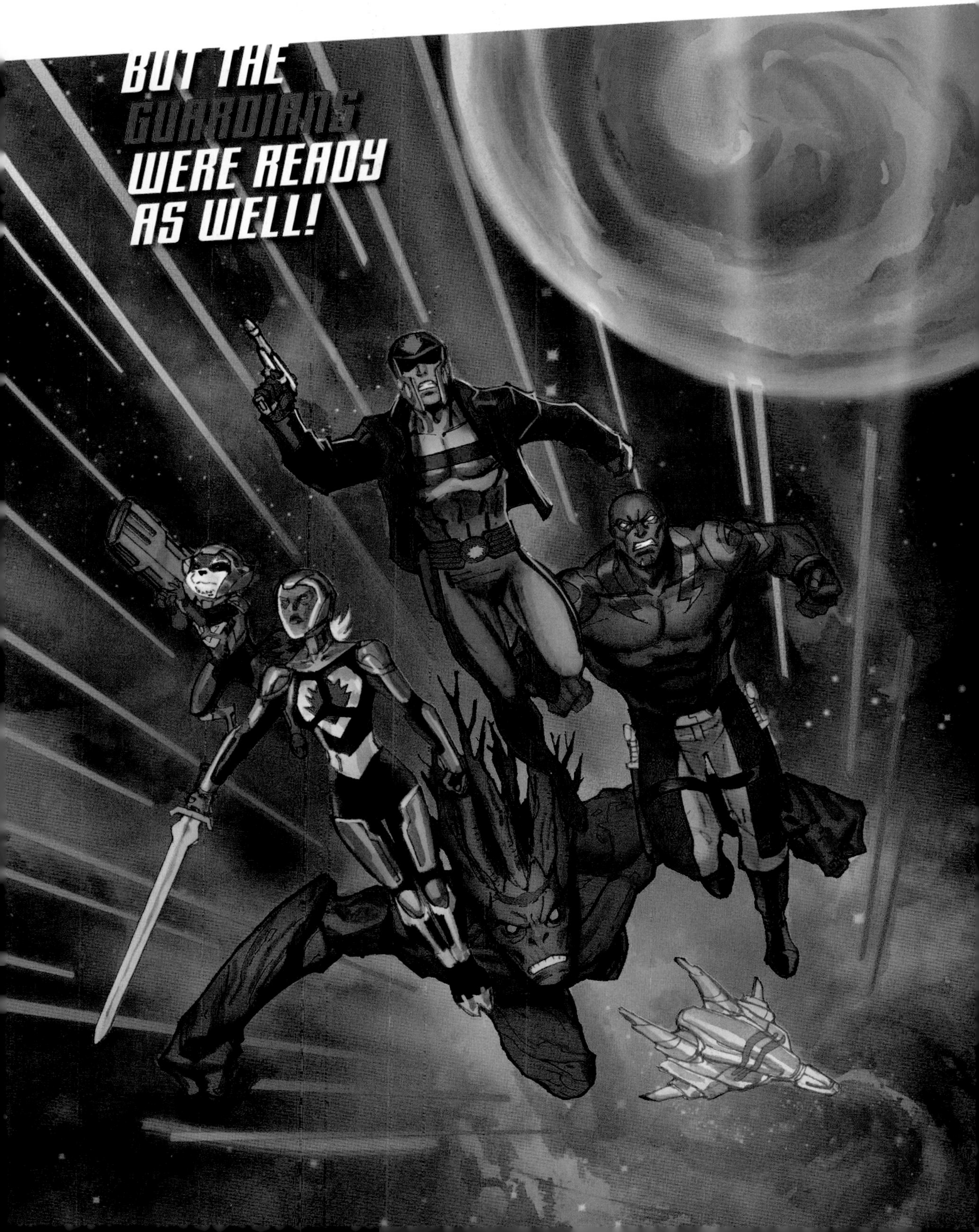
BUT THE GUARDIANS WERE READY AS WELL!

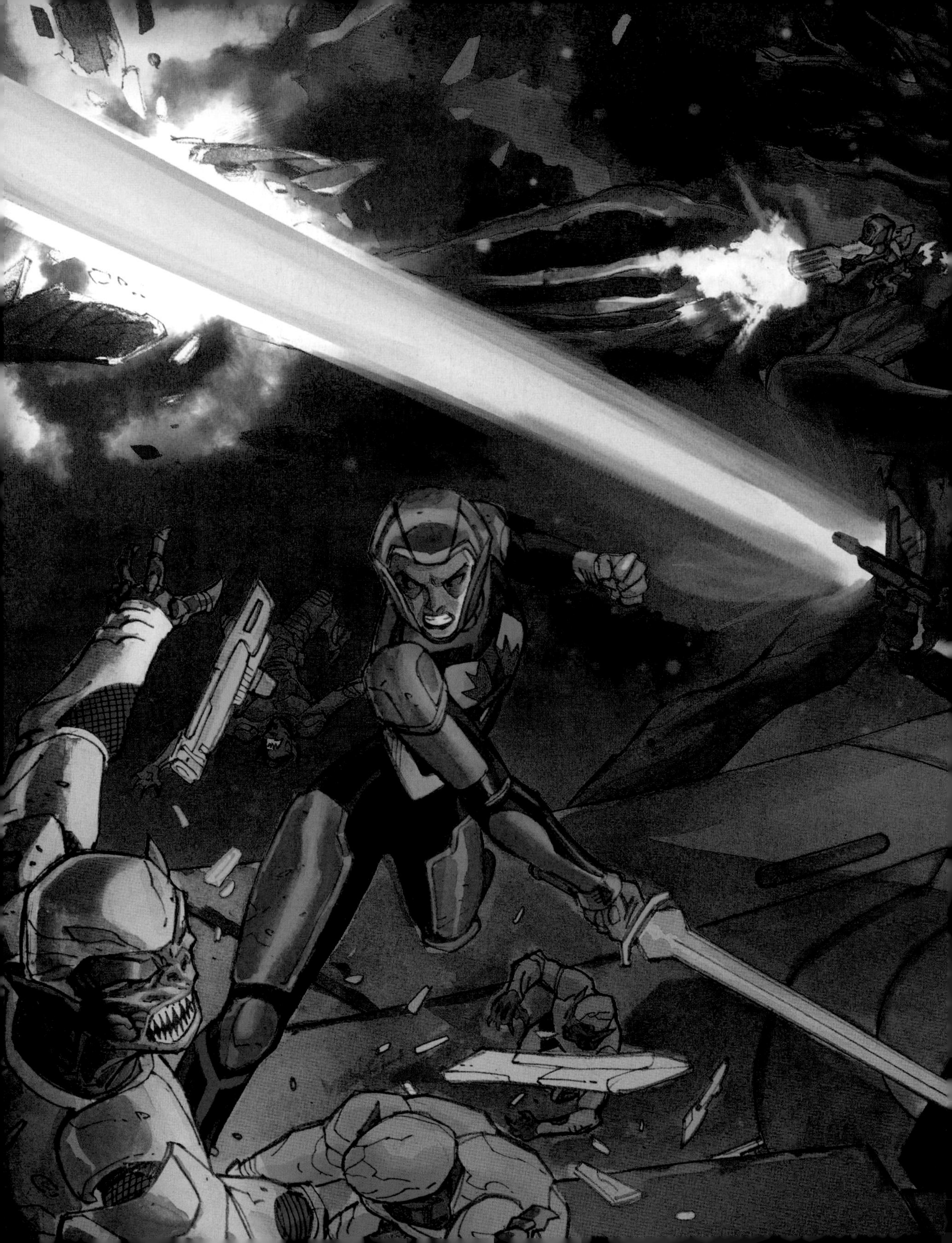

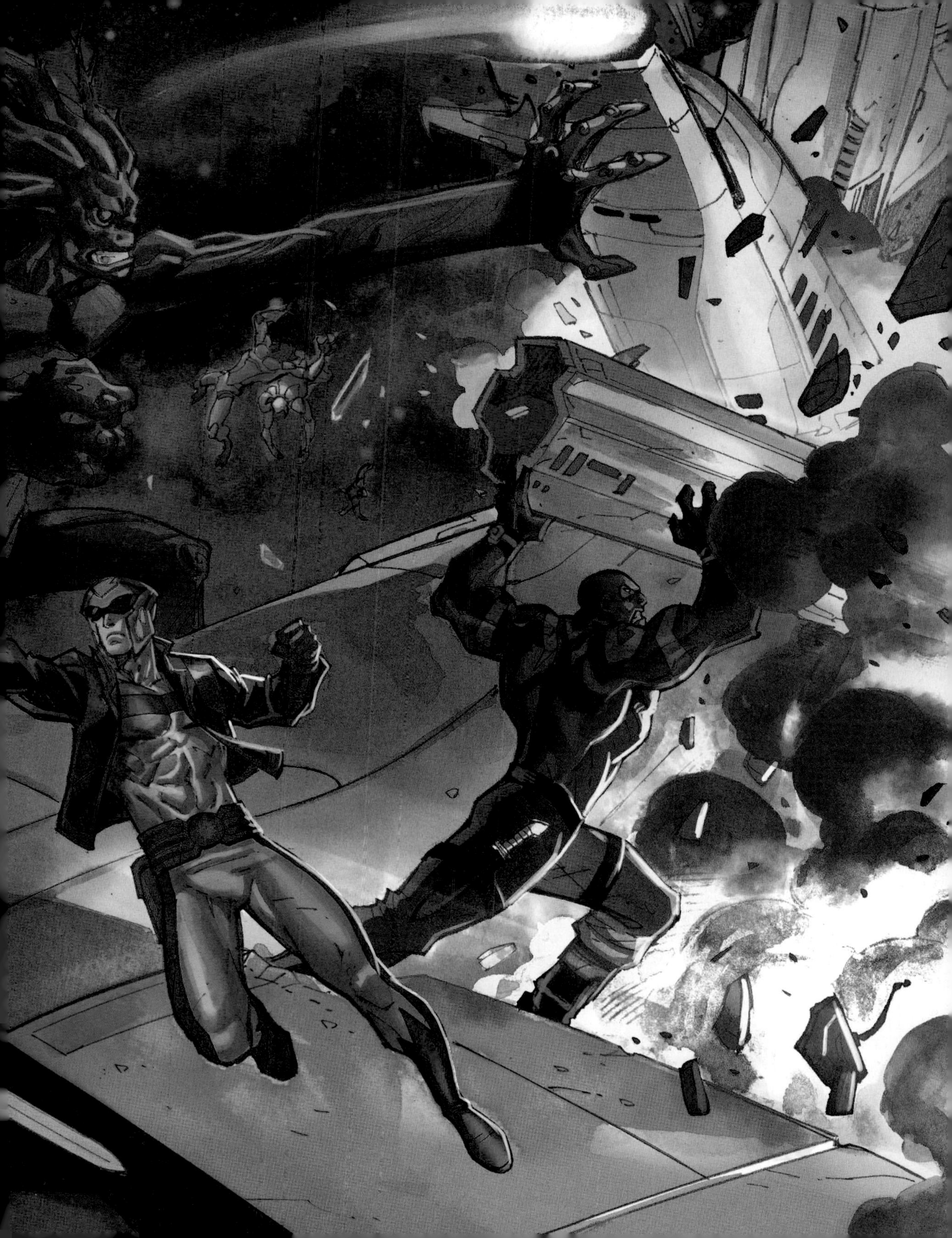

THE GUARDIANS FOUGHT WITH HEART, BATTLING LONG AND HARD.

Gamora, Drax, and Star-Lord worked as a team and tore through the Badoon with ease.

Groot grew and grew, towering over the Badoon, while Rocket used his arsenal of weapons to blast at the invading aliens.

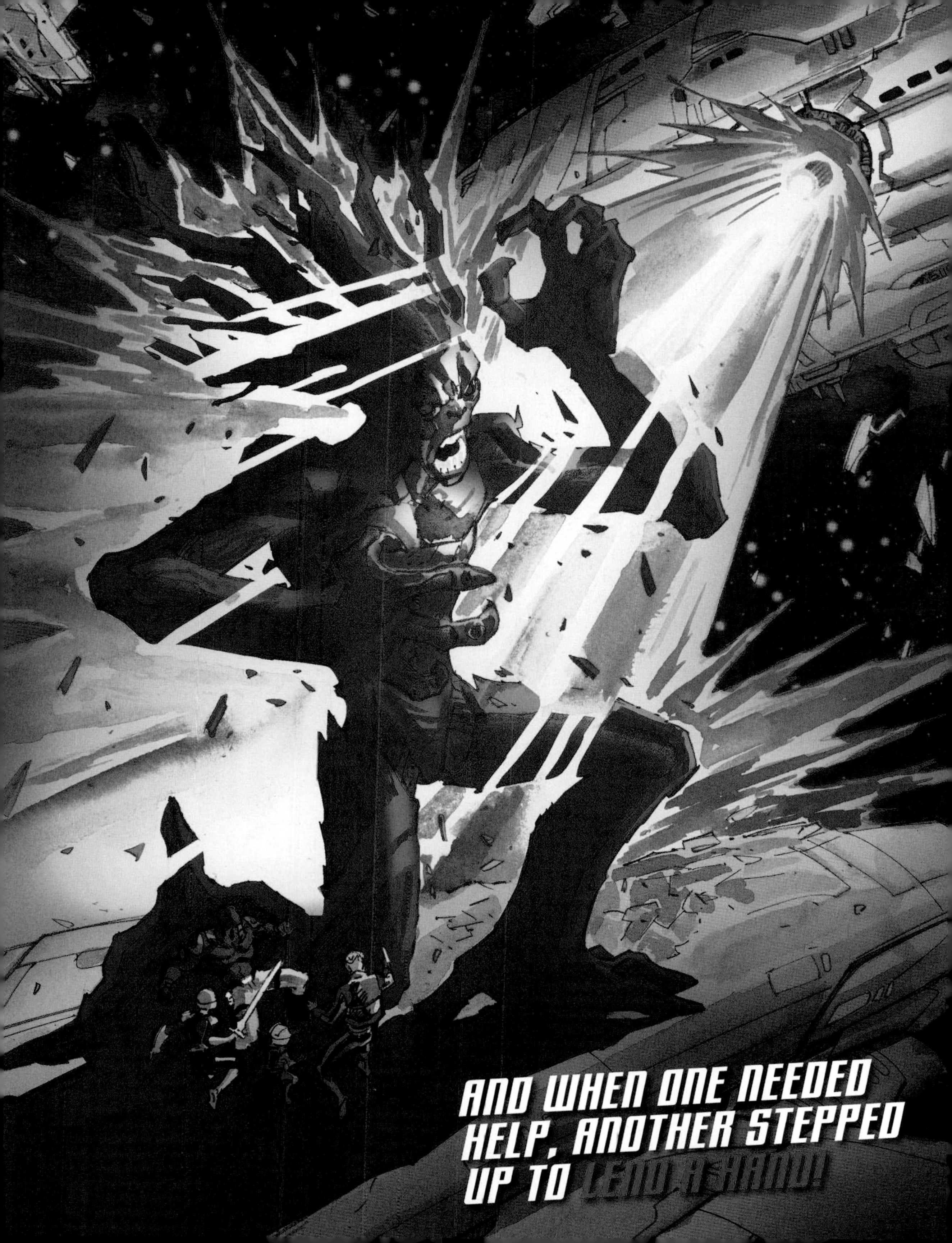
AND WHEN ONE NEEDED HELP, ANOTHER STEPPED UP TO LEND A HAND!

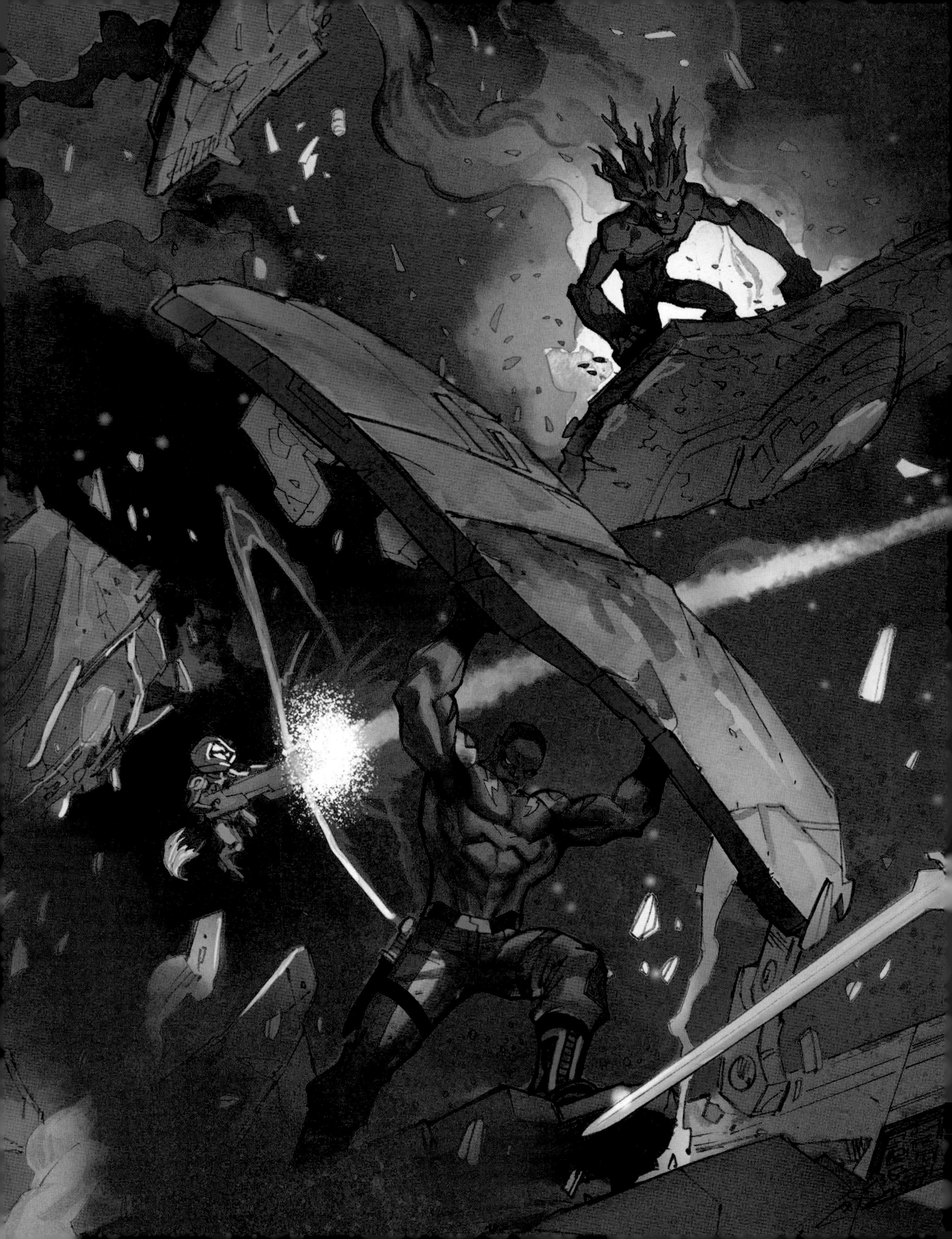

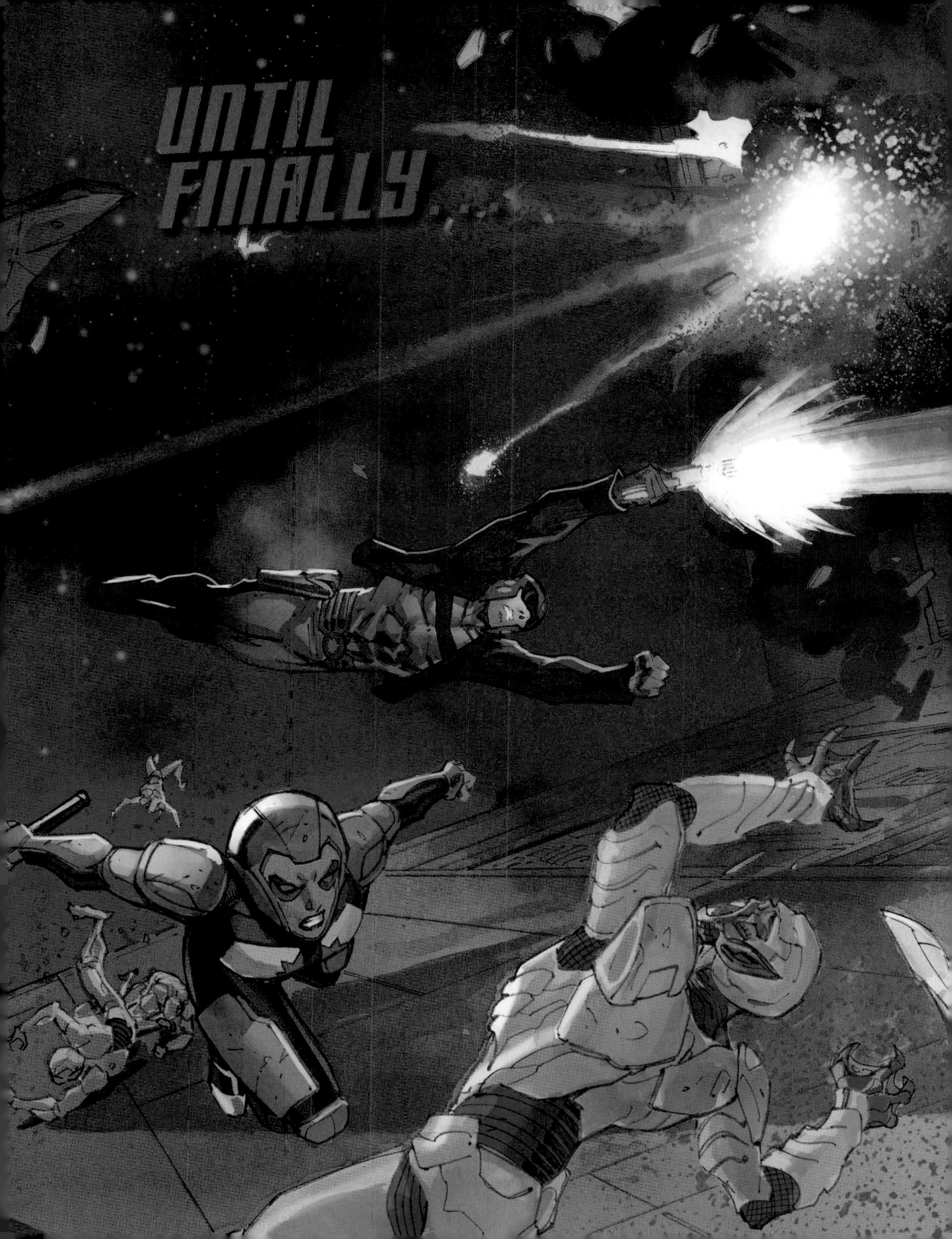
UNTIL FINALLY. . .

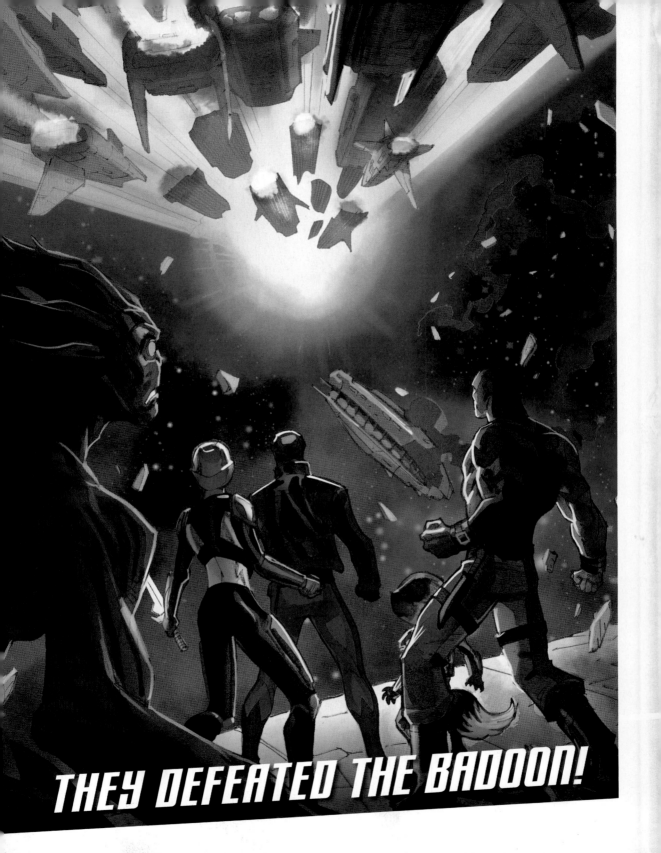

THEY DEFEATED THE BADOON!

Peter knew stopping the Badoon was a symbol of hope—for the galaxy, for Earth, for his friends and family.

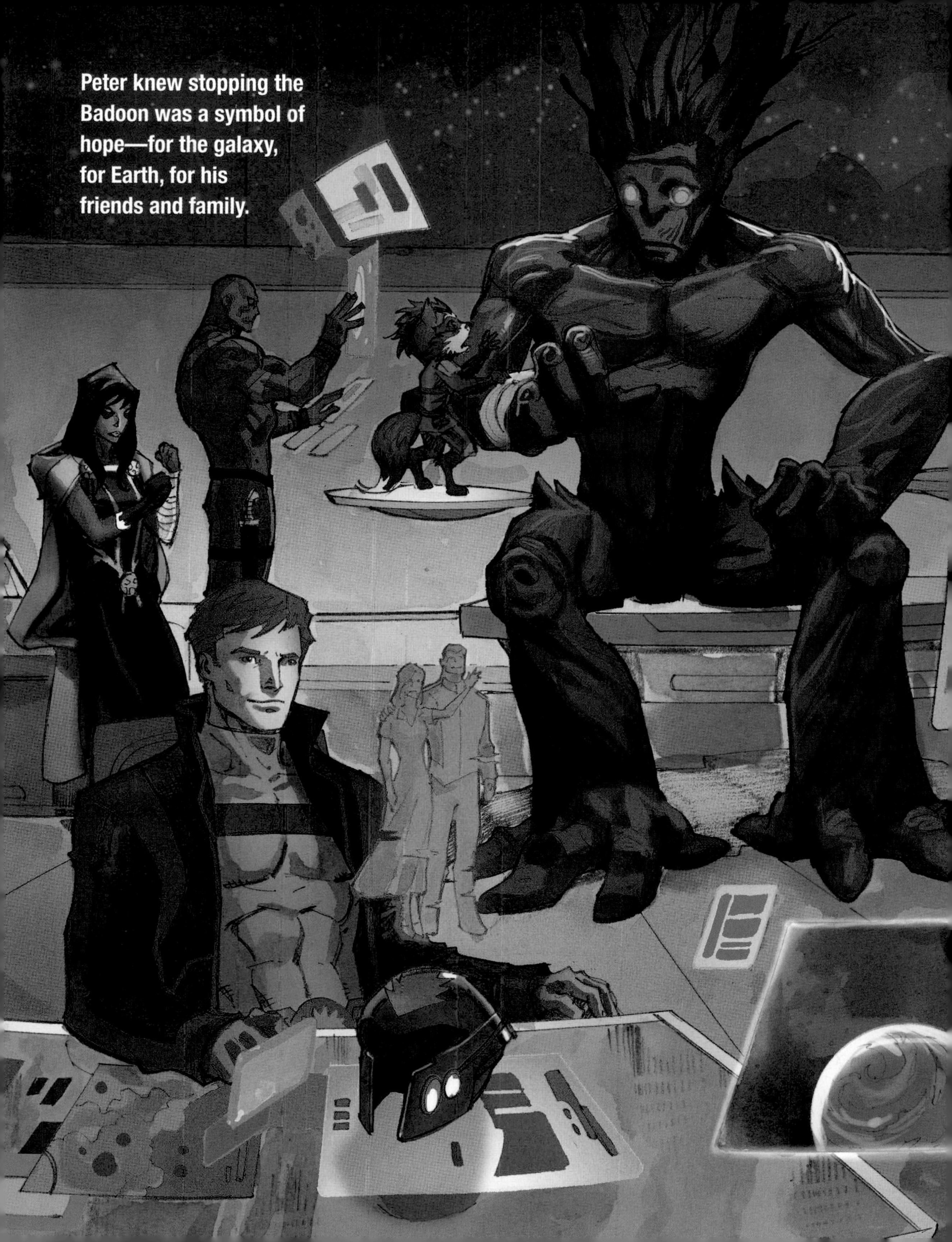

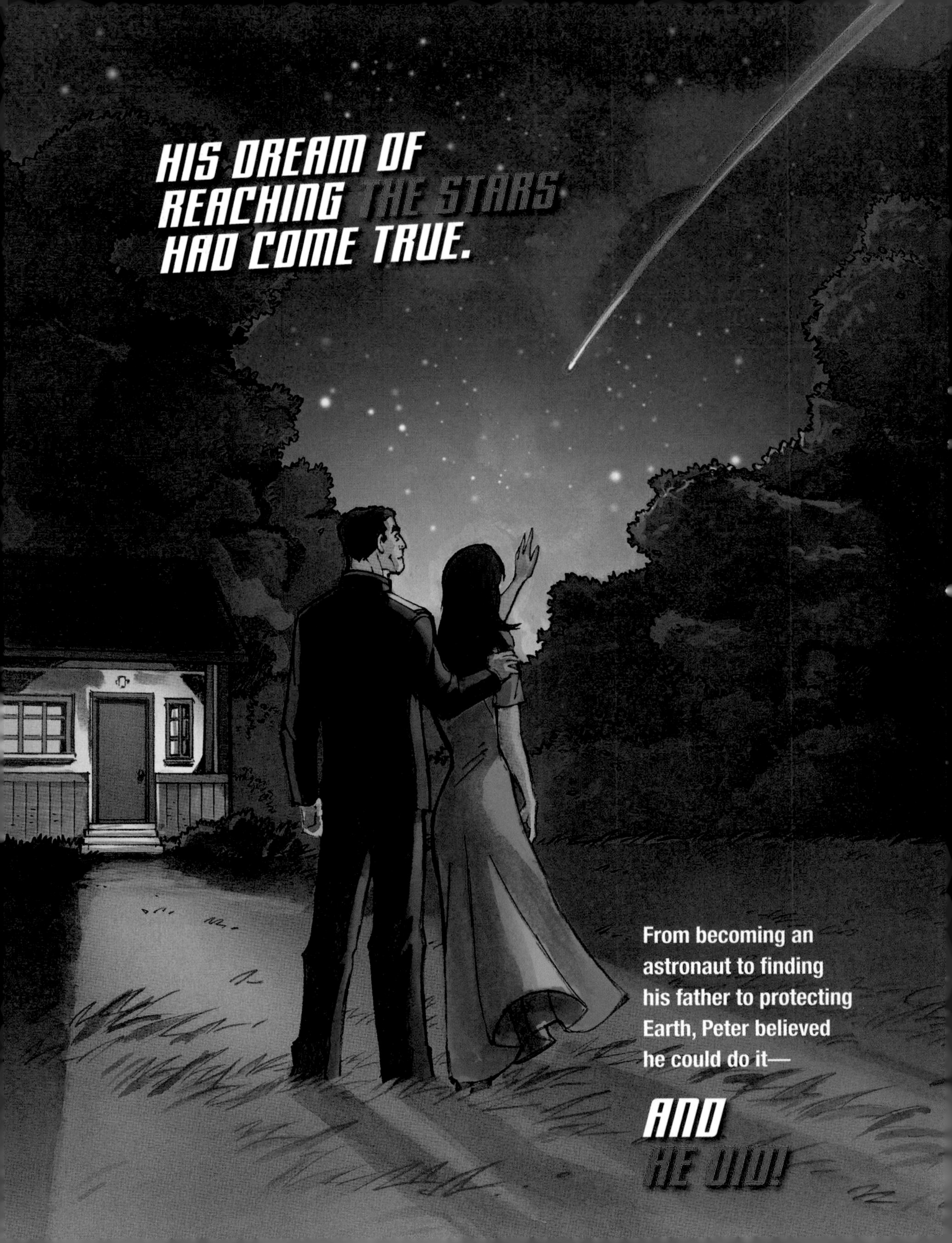
HIS DREAM OF REACHING THE STARS HAD COME TRUE.
From becoming an astronaut to finding his father to protecting Earth, Peter believed he could do it—
AND HE DID!

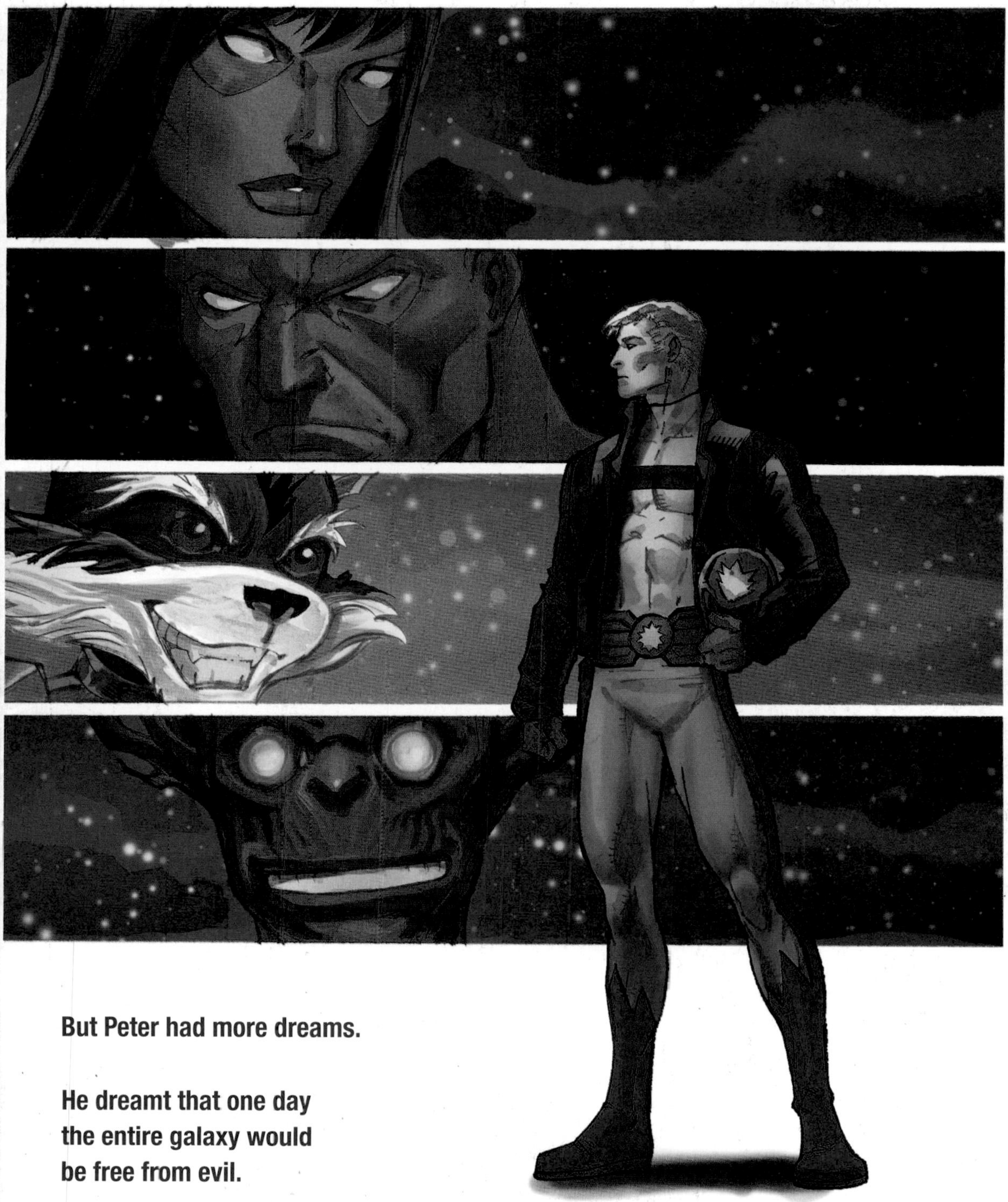

But Peter had more dreams.

He dreamt that one day
the entire galaxy would
be free from evil.

**GAMORA. DRAX. ROCKET. GROOT.
THEY TOO SHARED PETER'S DREAM.**

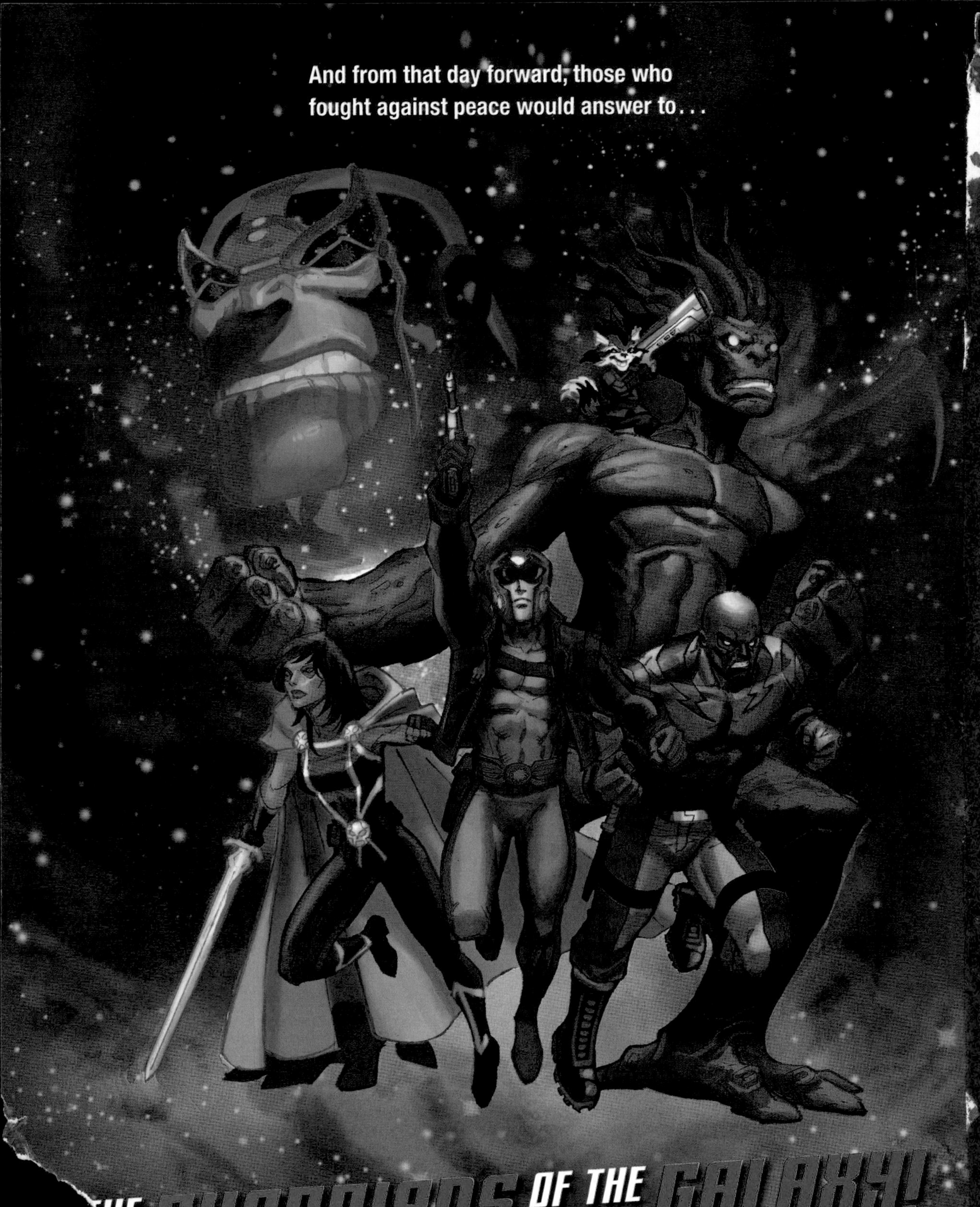
And from that day forward, those who fought against peace would answer to. . .
HE GUARDIANS OF THE GALAXY!